Theodore: The Neighbour's Cat

J.S Ellis

For information contact:

Black Cat Ink Press

https://blackcatinkpress.com/

J.S Ellis

https://www.joannewritesbooks.com

Cover Design by Milbart

Edited by Cecily Meyers Red Pen Editor

Proofread by Gem's Precise Proofreads

ISBN: Ebook 978-99957-1-775-9

Paperback: 978-99957-1-774-2

This book is written, edited and proofread in British English

Chapter one
Theodore

Hello, my name is Theodore. Before I get into my little story of mine, there are a few things you need to know about me; the first thing is that I am a cat. Before you laugh and dismiss me, I would like to tell you my story is quite a mouthful. I'm what humans call a Tuxedo cat, and I'm five years old. Yes, you can imagine how cute I look with my black and white coat and big doe green eyes. I live with Dean Carter. He hurts women. Have I piqued your interest now? In the period I have been his pet, he has killed four women and he's looking for the next one. Now, here, on this sunny little island called Malta. Dean got fed up with England, with its grey, damp weather, the lifestyle, how the country is being run and everything that goes with it. He decided we needed a little change. He was looking for somewhere different. Somewhere where the sun is warm, the sea is blue and the women are not just beautiful, but Mediterranean. Whatever he meant by that. If he killed before I came into his life, I don't know, but I suspect that he has.

I have tried to warn the four women he had elected. That's the word he uses: *elected*. However, I have failed to warn them. I'm in a bit of a pickle here; I'm limited to how much I can do and I can't exactly call for help. Humans are more superior when it comes to communication. We cats communicate with our tails and other body language. Cats form a great bond with their humans. Just like dogs do, we just express our affection differently. We are not cold; we're independent, magnificent and possess great hunting abilities, but we are loving affectionate creatures.

By no means am I subjected to cruelty. I am what one calls a content cat. Dean would never hurt me. I'm the only thing in his life that touches his human side, the soft side in him, so to speak. He feeds me twice daily, always high-quality brands. I drink water from a thing that flows water continuously. I think humans call it a fountain. He supplied it for me and I love it. My bowl of dry food is always full and he buys me toys to play with, although my favourite toy is the rod, and the patch of fluff that I tore off a particular toy. He gives me more treats than I would care to have and my litter is always clean. So, as you can see, I'm a spoiled boy. Despite Dean being who he is, I'm a happy little fellow. He cares about my wellbeing, but I dislike it when he takes me to the vet. He lets me go outside to play. He keeps the flat spotless. We felines are clean and we like our environment to be the same.

Let me tell you about Dean Carter. I often hear humans refer to my kind as sociopaths, but how? We are sensitive, we're soft, playful and we display emotions. We are not uncaring, neither selfish nor ungrateful. We are introverts who like our space. Dean is the sociopath, not me. Although he displays a lot of affection towards me, I don't want to think about how ruthless and vicious he can get. Dean is a quiet, reserved man. An ordinary man, living a normal life. At least, as normal as it can get. I'd like to think he's extremely handsome. I do like the sound of his voice, which is deep and rather husky, and I like his smell. He smells of warmth and comfort, which is the way to describe it. I like to think his looks are of an amiable quality when it comes to females. If only they stop, think and see him for who he truly is—a predator just like me. But a different kind of predator; it's a disease, he tells me. He likes to have conversations with me; I'm what you call his… confidant. I'm sure if these females would look hard enough, they would see something is not right about him. I think good looks are often conflicted with goodness and ugliness mistook for cruelty.

I think good-looking people take advantage of their position just like my human does. So, yes, Dean's looks might be a blessing, which makes this all too easy for him and more devastating for me.

In his defence, he doesn't kill each woman that comes to his path. He doesn't kill often, but he is a serial killer.

He chooses his victims carefully: ladies who fit a certain profile. Dean studies them. Gets to know about their lives, their habits. He doesn't get close to them or start a relationship with them or anything like that. He studies them from afar, and once he sees they have nothing else to offer or he gets bored with them, he kills them.

He had long-term relationships with the opposite sex and women have no idea what lies beneath his facade. Not that I blame them; he carries himself with them as he does with me, compliments them and gives them attention. How could they tell when he's so attentive, romantic, a gentleman and so good looking? He even fools me sometimes and I live with him. He's a cunning one, my Dean.

He had been married before, but the marriage ended in divorce; I don't know why it didn't last.

He draws a lot. He made a comic book based on me. Theodore The Magnificent, he called it. He hasn't published it; I'd be mortified if he does.

I didn't have a good start in life. I was born in England. I have six brothers and sisters. However, two months after our mum gave birth to us, the people she was living with didn't know what to do with us, so they found an easy solution to their problem by shoving us in boxes and dumping us in different locations around the area. It was raining and cold that night. I meowed and meowed, hoping my mum would come for me. Everything around me was dark. Footsteps approached, the box rattled a little before it opened, and a pair of blue eyes peered at me.

'Hello, there little fellow,' the man said. 'What happened to you?'

I meowed in response. He picked me up, put me inside his jacket and took me with him as if I belonged to him. He took me to his house and dried me with a towel. I was shaking and so he gave me water and food, which I didn't touch. The atmosphere was new to me and I didn't know this man. I was terrified. I wanted my mum, brothers and sisters.

I stared at him, at this man who rescued me and called himself Dean. I didn't think he intended to keep me. The next day, he picked me up - I was so small back then, I could fit in the palm of his hand. He gave me a long, hard look. I meowed and Dean smiled warmly at me. I would never have guessed this man could do such despicable things, not when he had such a sweet smile and a gentle face.

'Now, let's see what we're going to name you.' He went on inspecting me and his eyes widened.

'Theodore,' he said. 'You know your name has a biblical term.' he went on, holding me close to his heart. 'It means *God's Gift*."

Maybe I might not be such a thing, but I can be a gift to the next lady Dean set his eyes on.

Chapter Two
Theodore

I'm going to tell my tale as simply as humanly possible and everything I'm about to say, I have witnessed myself and some parts are what I've heard. Other parts are what Dean has told me. As I said before, Dean likes to talk to me. I presume since I don't talk back and I can't repeat anything he says, it makes it more convenient for him. We recently moved here, five months ago. I didn't like this change. Everything looks so peculiar. Cats do not take lightly to change. We're territorial animals, but I'm adjusting now, little by little. We live in a town called Hal-Balzan. It's August, and I like to bask under the sun, but in this heat, I'll be burned to a crisp. It can go up to 40 to 45 Celsius here and that is too hot. Dean finds it almost unbearable; he keeps applying a sort of cream on his fair skin. Last month, his skin went red as a lobster. Not even he knew how vicious the sun can be over here. He had been here before when he was a child, he told me. But the climate had changed, he had said. When we're inside, he switches on that white box on the wall and I hate it when the room gets cold, so I try to find a warm place away from that thing that spits cool air. Dean is on his laptop, designing something, or he's on the lookout. I can't tell which. He hasn't killed anyone on the island as of yet, but I don't know how long it's going to last.

Dean smiles down at me 'I'm going to run an errand. I'll be back soon okay, sausage?'

I go to the balcony. Clothes are hanging on the lines. In Malta, they hang clothes on the roof or balconies. A church bell is ringing in the distance. It's peaceful and quiet here and two women are on the pavement talking a bit loudly as if they are arguing, but that is how the Maltese talk—like they are fighting when they're just having a normal conversation. The bombastic women stop their loud chatter and their heads follow the tall, handsome young man walking past them. Dean smiles at them and greets them with a "good morning," all very civil and polite.

He puts on his sunglasses and the women turn pink as they say good morning back. They keep watching him until he disappears into a corner. Meanwhile, I lay down on the floor between the sun and the shadow and admire a house sparrow in one of the open vents.

In the evenings, Dean likes to sit outside to the balcony, to draw, and I'll keep him company. He's drinking from a can of local beer. Tonight, the air is humid, but there is a cool breeze tonight. Music is coming from the distance: trumpets and saxophones, which makes my sensitive ears go mad. I don't know why they do this over here, have these bands playing and parades in the street. I notice that it's only in the summer that there all of this noise. There is a clunk of a lobby door from across the street and a woman comes out. She's wearing a dress, but I can't say what colour; we're not blessed with the same colour schemes that humans have. She's tall and slim. Her hair is wavy and dark. Dean's eyes lift from the pad. He's about to go back to his work, but does a double-take. I stand on alert. He places the pencil down and drinks the woman in. She's standing right across from us with her hands folded across her chest, tapping her feet impatiently as if she's waiting for someone. The lobby door does another clunk and a man follows. Dean's full attention is on them now as the woman says something to the man in a raspy voice. I meow to distract Dean, but he lifts his hand as if to tell me to be quiet. I go cold. The couple walks on as the woman links her arm through her partner's. There is a content smile on her face, as if she's in her right happy place, and Dean's eyes have penetrated through her.

'What do you think, Theodore?' Dean asks after the couple disappear out of sight.

I stare at him.

'I have to find out who she is.'

There she is: the next victim he's about to prey on. He's about to get to work and I have to do the same.

The women Dean has elected before didn't have companions, but this one does. This will be a bit more difficult for him as this requires more work. That is good news for me; it gives me more time. Someone worries about her and misses her. He has a special kind of criteria for the women he elects, Dean has told me they need to have dark hair, have successful careers, who strictly do not have companions, who strictly do not have too many friends, who strictly do not post a lot on that place people post photos or share their thoughts. I think I heard Dean refer to it as *social media*. Facebook, Instagram and Twitter. I like the last name best; it sounds like a bird.

If this woman is Dean's next target, I have to act or else her life would end tragically like the rest.

Dean and I are out on the balcony (I'm basking under the sun and he's drinking from a bottle of cold beer) when her companion arrives home. He carries a black case with him. Dean's eyes are set on the man. He has a cold look on his face. Does he have something planned already? Is her companion a potential target? I don't want this lady to die. I don't want her companion to die either. Why can't Dean stop? Why can't he put an end to it? I hate that he hurts other people.

The lady is out on the balcony sneaking a cigarette. When she sees her companion open the lobby door, she throws the cigarette out and goes inside, sliding the door behind her. Dean slides our door closed and looks down at me.

'You know what I found today, little fellow? Her name is Jane, she's a crime writer and that man is her husband... for now.'

What does he mean by for now? He gets on with his work. His work—that's what he likes to call it—involves lots of time and patience. He has both.

I like writers; they create things and lift people's imagination. Jane doesn't have the slightest notion she's starring in one of her own stories as the would-be main murder victim.

'Her husband name is Matthew, apparently. She mentioned him in one of her Instagram posts."

Dean bought all of Jane's books. I think he's trying to discover more about her by reading her stuff. Jane sounds too good to be true. How has Dean found someone so amazing? It's like she dropped from the sky to our street especially for him. Dean is working on something major, and this fills me with so much dread.

As my human has a plan, so do I. I have to get close to her. I'm the only friend she has without knowing, her only ally of what's about to come, and I have to find a way to warn her somehow. The *how,* I'm not sure I have established yet. It's not like I can knock on her door and tell her. She goes out - not sure where, and Dean sometimes follows her. To learn more about her, of course. To get an idea of how she spends her day. Since she's so interesting, he might give her more time, unlike the rest. Maybe I should go on those adventures myself and see where she goes, to know more about her, but I can't risk Dean seeing me. Although, I have an advantage when it comes to hiding. I don't think he'll mind; he knows I can't do much in this situation. He might find the whole prospect of me following her as well amusing. But unlike Dean, I'll do it for the greater good.

One day, as part of my daily stroll, I go near the block of flats she lives in. There are other cats in the neighbourhood. There is a lady who owns eight cats and a few strays are lurking about. I do not interact with these cats. I keep myself to myself. I'm reserved, like Dean. The lobby door opens and Jane comes out. She's wearing large sunglasses with frames so black I can hardly see her eyes. She's dressed in a baggy dress and her hair is up in a bun, which makes me want to play with it. Jane stops dead in her tracks and slaps her hand against her cheeks. I'm licking my paw but stop and look at her, then I go on with my grooming session as if I can't be bothered, as if she holds no importance to me.

'What a dumpling! You're wearing socks!' she squeals, pointing at my white paws.

I blink at her. Dean is not the only handsome fellow in this neighbourhood. I glance at her.

'Hello there, potato,' she says waving her hand at me as if I can wave back. She checks her watch.

'Oh, shoot, I'm already late,' she says. 'I would love to stay and worship you but I must run. Bye, sweetie.'

And with that, she walks off. I have established the first step: she acknowledges me, doesn't hate cats nor is terrified of me. This is a good thing.

Chapter Three
Dean

I watch him, this cat of mine. Does he know I am the man women fear even though I'm swathed in gentleness? They fear me without knowing they have to. I am unseen. I don't break into their homes, but I make accidents happen. I am invisible. Is this bundle of joy aware of that? I watch Theodore and he watches me. We always watch each other. He's like a reflection of me. A mirror. He came to me like a gift. Wrapped and delivered to me in a wet shoebox tossed aside to die. I was walking down the street in London in a darkened alleyway when I found him. Some people get scared walking in those kinds of alleys; you can run into all sort of things in places like those. Mostly teenagers trying to be proper naughty boys. I came across one once, he pointed a gun at me, demanding I should give him my wallet, phone and other valuables I was carrying. I lifted my hand in surrender and he made me go by the wall. As I faced the wall, I thought about what I could do to that kid. Who was the proper naughty boy among us? It wasn't him, but he didn't have to know that. He searched my leather jacket and found my wallet and my phone. I remained quiet. He continued to look for another valuable; I wasn't going to let anyone hold me at gunpoint and mug me. With my elbow, I hit him in the stomach, and with the surprise, the gun thudded to the ground. I turned and punched him so hard, I knocked his front teeth out. It was a bold move. I could have been shot. I gave the kid a little talk while I collected my valuables, took the gun (which I threw in the river) and left him there collecting his teeth.

You can say I look for trouble, that I'm addicted to risk and danger, and I am. I kill to see if I can get away with it, and I do. I also kill because I have to. We all have evil inside of us, it's stagnant and waiting, it grows in us like a cancer but only if you feed it what it wants our hate and anger. Some of us give in to that hate and anger.

One night, I was walking down another alley and this time, I heard the mewling of a cat in distress. I kept on walking, but I stopped and thought I should look for it. By the mewling echoing through the walls, I could tell it wasn't a fully-grown cat, but a kitten. It felt like he was calling out to me.

Help me, help me, please help. Please save me. Don't leave me here.

I found a shoebox near a dumpster wet from the rain. That night, I was on my way home after the pub and fate had led me to find this poor little fellow. Better than being held at gunpoint, I suppose. I opened the box and the first thing I saw were those green eyes looking at me with distrust. I made out the black and white coat. The white paws at its front and back legs as if he was wearing shoes. His tail was all black apart from the tip, which was white. The kitten meowed again. It was tiny, maybe no more than two months old. It was shaking with the cold or fear, or both. I wondered what sort of monster would abandon such a helpless, adorable tiny thing like that out in this cold, leaving it to die. I am a monster, but not the sort that would hurt an animal. That is unacceptable. *How many kittens have a bad start in their lives?* I asked myself as I held the kitten up, who was scared and defenceless. I couldn't leave him there. No, this baby boy will be cherished and adored. He was unwanted, but it didn't have to be that way. I would take him with me, give him food and shelter. If I left him there, he wouldn't have made it through the night. He'd be my little companion. A friend who would understand me. I put him inside my jacket for warmth. When I was a child, we had a white cat named Skittles. I always found cats to be such stimulating companions. I admire them for their excellent hunting skills. How alert they are. How they observe each tiny detail. Always watching. I also admired their elegance and how they carried themselves with such grace. Cats are such beautiful, fascinating creatures, and since I'm a hunter myself, it was logical to own another hunter. The perfect companion.

When I took him home, I dried him and gave him water, but I had nothing for him to eat. So I rushed to the twenty-four-hour market down the road and bought some cat food and tuna. The kitten ignored me; he hid under the chair and I gave him his space, but he watched me, never took his eyes off me. The next morning, I looked at him while he drank and ate. He looked at me as he licked his lips. I noticed his nose was pink and my heart melted. It was impossible to say no to him. I found him for a reason. He was a gift and I was going to keep him.

I picked him up and inspected this miraculous little guy. He meowed, then placed his pink paw on my nose.

'Very cute,' I said to him. 'We should give you a name, don't you agree, little guy? What shall we name you… let's see…'

He was a gift, and the name Theodore sounded fitting. A Greek name that means God's Gift.

I didn't think I was capable of love. He's the only living thing who can make me feel something close to emotions. He sits there and waits to be worshipped. Sometimes, however, it looks like this cat can see straight through me, this guardian of the underworld, this regal protector, but all he does is take naps.

I got fed up with London and with all that had been going on lately; it was too mundane. I figured a change would do us good. I am careful, vigilant, and alert. I have to be, given what I do; I can't afford to be sloppy. Sloppiness and impatience are what get killers caught in the first place, or the pattern gets old. Or they get cocky and start to kill more frequently. I will not make that mistake. I wonder if sometimes if the police can sniff me up, but that is unlikely, but not impossible.

I remember when my parents took my brother and me to Malta when we were children, and the place stayed with me. We used to spend hours playing on the sand. Malta, although not free from crime, it isn't exposed to serial killers. Well, one killed three elderly pensioners in their homes during a robbery in the '80s and throughout the

'90s. If for the Maltese standards, he was considered a serial killer, what did that make me? Malta is a quiet little land, enough for me to seek and kill without being sniffed, but it doesn't mean I can be cocky. As soon as I landed, I was hit by the change. The sky was blue, not even a cloud in the sky compared to the grey moody English weather. It was April when I moved, but it felt like the UK summer. Everything looked different, with colourful balconies and doors. Malta is an island of culture and history.

I bought a flat in Hal-Balzan, a modest enough neighbourhood. It's not a tourist place on the island, not like Sliema or St. Julian's, or the capital city Valletta. There is a big posh hotel not far from here, but still, it doesn't attract that many tourists. I work as a freelance illustrator and I work from home. I had saved up plenty of money in my years. I always have been careful with money and how much I spend. Although, I do like to care of myself, especially my hair: light brown and styled in the greaser rebel sort of way, like a '50s reject, so it needs plenty of up keep.

You might walk past me in the street and I might even attract your attention as you see me over six feet tall with sharp features and high sculptured cheekbones, a long nose and piercing blue eyes, and you might think to yourself, 'Now that's a good looking man'. I can hide my coldness, smile warmly with you, engage in a conversation and make you laugh, but when I look in the mirror, I don't see me, because there is no me. All I see is nonentity. An illusory, so to speak.

When I moved here, I didn't take anything from my old life with me. Instead, I bought everything new for a new life. My flat is spacious, possibly too large for a man and a cat. The décor is modern with white walls and abstract pictures hanging on them. White marble floors, a black leather sofa, which I keep covered so Theodore doesn't dig his claws into it. There isn't much furniture apart from the coffee table and the wall unit for the TV. There are large vases decorating the corners of the rooms and a cabinet by the front door where I put my keys and wallet. The kitchen, which I use quite frequently, is modular and it's black and white. The bedroom has more cushions than a boutique hotel and it makes the room look 'nice and warm'. Warm. Now that is a word that doesn't describe me at all. I would describe the apartment as a beautiful, chic museum of a place, but what I wouldn't tell them is how much it reflects my personality. There is a certain coldness to it, devoid of soul.

Theodore didn't take the move lightly; he had been irritable, although now, he seems to be content in his little world.

To my dismay, as I began to explore, the island was no longer how I remembered it. The change had been rather drastic: the beach where I used to play is now a monstrosity of a shopping mall and a complex for the rich arseholes to accommodate themselves and their wealth. The beach is still there, but it's not the same. The charm is gone. The churches are built with the highest peaks here, part of the Maltese's charm. These churches are grandiose with the interior decorated with fine art, gold and velvet tapestries. That was then. Now the highest peaks are no longer those churches that dominated the skyline and demanded attention, but the cranes. Such a shame. All of this for the rich to fill their pockets with gold.

I spotted a few potential candidates during my move here, but there was always something wrong. Either they were too popular, which is never good, post too much on social media, which is another problem, or have partners. Although not a major threat, still a problem. I look for people who won't be missed and can die in accidental deaths. Something plausible. Not to make the police suspect anything or track something back to me. The problem with knives, guns, axes and whatever you can deem as a weapon is that they leave too much evidence. This time, however, I'm looking for something different. Not sure what exactly, but I will find out as I always do.

Chapter Four
Theodore

Dean doesn't notice I go out longer than usual. Or if he is aware, given how alert he is, he doesn't mind. He monitors how long I stay out and come back. I'm trying to establish a connection with Jane, but she's staying in more than usual. I sit by her apartment and wait, hoping she'd come out. I saw her a few times looking out to the balcony and she saw me. I wonder if she finds the whole prospect of me sitting outside her apartment strange. When I come back home, Dean is on the phone, his cheeks are red and from his tone, he doesn't sound happy.

'Well, I don't care,' he snarls.

I pad to the sofa; his laptop is lying there next to papers and a pen with some software open.

'What do you want me to do from here? No, I no longer live there. It's not your bloody business where I live now,' he retorts to the receiver.

It must be his ex-wife on the other end. I don't know why they keep in touch; human relationships are so strange to me. The way they behave. How they treat each other. Every time she calls, he gets upset.

Dean slams the phone down and this startles me.

'Bitch,' he mutters under his breath.

He huffs, puffs and slumps down on the sofa, fingers tapping with impatience. Dean quickly stands, goes to the fridge and takes out a bottle of beer. He sits back down on the sofa and glances at me. I watch him in earnest. His face softens. I go to him, rubbing my head against his thigh, and I purr. I get a stroke on the ear for my effort. He scribbles something on his notepad and gives me another stroke.

'Our neighbour is a creature of habit,' he tells me, 'but I want to know more about her.'

He has a plan of attack. If only I know what. My purrs increase with anxiety now. What does he plan to do? Go after her and attack her? But that is unlike him. Well, I can't say what is unlike him or not. He never attacked the women he elected in my presence, never brought the victims to his home, but he does bring women here, the ones he mates with.

When does he plan to make this move? What if he gets caught? What if someone sees him? I know how he operates, though; he's sleek and wise. It has to be something undetected. Something that doesn't raise an alarm. An accident of some sort that Jane would think it was her being sloppy. But she's a writer, and she has to be as organised as he is. Aren't writers always studying their environment to formulate a story around them? He never gets close to the elected ones until he makes his final move.

At night is when I'm the most vulnerable, so I like to stay close to Dean because I trust him and I like to keep warm. I love the heat of my human. Also whatever evil will come to us, we can fight it together. Tonight, however, Dean is not here to fight the evil forces with me. He's out somewhere and he's been gone a long time. I wonder where he went. I saw Jane go out and a few minutes later, he followed. I hop off the bed and go to the balcony, but the door is closed. I sit and watch, trying to make out a sense of the ripples and the faint sounds. I have a bad feeling about this; did he do what he had planned? I hate not knowing. He wouldn't attack her here, not in the neighbourhood. Flats and houses surround the street. Cars are always rumbling by or parking in the garage below. There are other cats, too: a Siamese cat in his basket licking his paw, a stray lying on a car roof. None of them but me seem to hear anything. All the cats are going about their business. Maybe I imagined it, or maybe I dreamt it. Now I can't be sure. I linger by the sliding door; a fly is going downwards then upwards on the window. I try to catch it until I realise it is on the other side where I can't reach it—just like I can't reach Jane. A few minutes later, the front door opens and the lights blare the apartment alight. I run to the door as if to greet him, more curious than anything else. Dean's chest is puffing in and out as if he ran all the way here, and my heart sinks. He did it. He went out there and *did it*. Whatever it is. I keep my tail low to show him I'm worried, but Dean ignores me and proceeds to the sofa, producing a phone with a red cover. He taps on the screen. I climb next to him and he continues tapping. I don't know if this phone belongs to Jane or not, but he's so keen on her, I presume it to be hers. Now what? And how did he manage to take it in the first place? What if it can be tracked?

The curtains in her apartment are wide open; it's not normal for her to leave the curtains like that. She and Matthew are private people. Jane is sitting on the sofa with her legs tucked under her. I glance back at Dean, who looks pleased with himself. My handsome human is capable of so many bad things, and yet all people see is the front he displays, not the interior where his true ugliness lies. Matthew is on his feet with his hands on his hips, looking deeply concerned. Jane places her hand over her head while talking, getting angrier by the minute. Matthew raises his hand as if to calm her down. She reaches for a packet of tobacco and starts rolling a cigarette. Matthew says something to her and she flips her hand up to dismiss him. Jane smokes with her eyes averted to the floor. Dean walks over and picks me up. I purr. He thinks it's because I'm content, but it's the anxiety that makes me purr. Mathew has bought her a glass of water, which Jane doesn't touch but finishes the cigarette. He opens his arms. She stands, and they embrace.

'Jesus, the guy doesn't even bother to hug her. She has to stand to receive it. Is this some kind of Maltese mentality?' Dean grumbles to me and moves away from the window.

We lay in the dark, me purring, him with his brain ticking, gathering ideas, unable to let him rest. I can almost see them, the lightbulbs flashing over his head.

Chapter Five
Dean

I don't come from a rough background. My parents weren't abusive or anything like that. My father didn't beat my mother, nor were they alcoholics. They didn't neglect me or my brother. I didn't have non-family members abusing me, either. Nothing of that sort. We had a normal upbringing and came from a stable background. My parents worked hard to earn us an education, to put food on the table and clothes on our backs. We had a good childhood, holidays every year or so. How did I become like this? Even I sometimes wonder. I think I was born this way. A defect of some sort. My brother Steve is a broker; he's five years older than me. We speak occasionally, but not often. The last time I spoke to him, which was about a month ago, he said he's dating a girl whose name I can't remember. They don't last long enough to remember their names anyway. He's more in a relationship with his job than the women he dates. They are more like additions where they join him in events or public gatherings. *Escorts* is the right word. We don't have a strained relationship; we're just busy. As for my parents, my mum used to be a doctor, now retired, and my father taught art, now also retired. He taught me and my brother how to draw, but Steve was never interested in arts and drawings. But for me, it was like flowers blooming on a summer's day. I speak to my parents once a week through video calls. They were surprised when I told them I was going to move to live elsewhere, but not shocked; I guess they knew I would do it somehow.

'Live elsewhere? Where?' my mum asked, her eyes wide.

'Malta,' I said.

'Oh, that is a lovely place, but wouldn't you be lonely?' my dad asked.

'I will manage,' I said.

Dad opened a door for me in the direction of what I wanted to do with my life. I wanted to do something that would allow me to do what I love while earning a sustainable income, but I wasn't sure what yet. When I turned sixteen, things took a turn to the dark, and for some, disturbing. I guess sixteen is the age when you start to get to know yourself. The age that defines you, in a way. I didn't care much for self-destruction, but I had my kind of rebellion: something that wouldn't show, hidden for only myself to see. I used to watch girls strolling by, but instead of wondering what colour their panties were, I pictured how they would look like as corpses. I used to draw dead girls during history lessons - my least favourite subject. These drawings consisted of girls with cracked skulls and their brains scattered all over the ground after they fell to their deaths, or girls pushed into an oncoming bus. I drew what was lurking at the back of my mind; it was like a monster was yowling and seething within me, another version of myself scratching within me waiting to be unleashed. Little did I know back then that I would recreate these drawings in real life.

A few doors down from where I lived, there was a woman who was older than me. I think she was in her late twenties and always stayed at home in her dressing gown. I don't think I ever saw her leave the house. She used to linger by the front door of her house smoking a cigarette. Her husband had died a few years back from a car accident. She used to watch me walk by, and I would awkwardly nod in her direction and keep on going. One day, as I walked past her house, she was outside smoking and started a conversation. She asked me questions about where I went to school, that sort of thing. She was pretty with long brown hair and hazel eyes with low cheekbones and a slightly upturned nose. The chats were friendly and they went on for about a month or so. Her name was Ann and she was the beginning of everything; she shaped me to be the man I am now, what I have become, but she wasn't to blame. I was the architect of my own making. One afternoon, Ann invited me to her house, offered me tea, and told me that I was very good looking. She asked me what I thought of girls. Ann took my hand, led me to her bedroom, and explained to me what she wanted me to do to her. I wanted to run away, but something in me twitched when she disrobed and took off her underwear and laid on the bed, waiting for me to make my move. That urge, that monster inside me, growled.

'Haven't you been with a woman before?' she asked.

'Err… no,' I replied.

She smiled and stood from the bed. I gazed at her generous breasts and the dark hairs between her legs.

'Don't worry,' she purred, 'I'll teach you everything about how to please a woman.'

I was surprised I could do that to a woman. Give her that kind of pleasure, to make her want me like that. All the while as I did it to her, I wondered what it would be like to wrap my hands around her neck and suck the life out of her. To watch the light from her eyes disappear, and the last thing she saw would be the gentleness of my face.

I had fed on that urge; Ann was the first woman I had been with and the first woman I killed. Nobody asked questions; nobody cared about a widowed woman who didn't have any family to worry about her. The police didn't, either. She fell down the stairs and I was the cause. I watched how her body was angled in a strange position as if it was twisted, how her neck was broken. To this day, it still surprises me how simple it all had been: Ann had too much wine and slipped. Case closed.

I had cried that day more than I cried in my life. I was disgusted with myself. So much so that I almost went to the police station. I did go. I stood outside the building, contemplating if I should go in or not and confess what I had done.

'Hey, mate, are you alright?' a man called out.

I turned and it was a uniformed police officer. I swallowed the bile that raised from my stomach. This was my chance. I could tell him what I had done.

'Yes,' I replied.

He looked at me hard as if he could tell I'd done something by looking at me. I had shoulder-length hair back then, wore jeans and oversized jumpers.

'Are you sure?' he asked.

I nodded.

'Then be on your way, mate. We have things to do,' he said.

I didn't confess when the chance had presented itself so easily. I doubted that the officer would have believed me either way. What proof did I have? The police never came to question me. Neighbours could have seen me going into her house. But nobody gave a shit. Everyone is too wrapped in their own bubble to care. After all, it looked like an accident. I got away with it. I laid on my bed that night and thought about what I had done, it was as if I was a snake peeling off his skin. I thought of the power it gave me. I could control if someone should live or not. It was like playing God. A pattern started to form in my head that would be the map for my later life.

Her name is Jane Cassar. I found this out when one of the bombastic neighbours called out for her as Jane was coming back from her shopping. That night, I snuck by her apartment and looked at the surnames on the letterboxes. I went to the bar for a drink; I looked up her on Google.

This is what I found out so far, thanks to social media; Jane is thirty years old - three years older than me. She's a crime writer, the irony, and has published twelve books. She has plenty of reviews under her belt. There are a mix of 5, 4, 3, and a few 2 and 1 stars. I start by reading the low ratings first. With the internet as wonderful as it is, it gives people the power to act as if they are experts. But art is subjective: one says how great it is, the another says it's a load of bollocks. They are just opinions. I buy all her books. From what I have read so far, (a book titled *Into The Cold*, which is part of a five book series following a detective trying to solve a murder) it's good. I mean it's not *War and Peace* or anything like that, but engaging enough and well-written.

Our Jane doesn't like to be seen, unlike most people these days, where everyone is striving for attention. *Look at me. Look how fabulous my life is!* But nobody airs their dirty laundry online. Living to collect likes and comments. And we're spending more time tapping and tapping into our phones, tablets, ATMs that we forgot what it feels like to hold an actual pen or write on paper. Seriously, when did the world become this fucked? Since when have people become so bloody uptight and get offended by every little thing? These posts on social media, the tweets, the selfies especially, are a sign of insecurities, low self-esteem and quite frankly, a gesture of hate. Yes, this is rich coming from a cold, sadistic bastard like me. I wonder - are we truly evolving as human beings or are we going backwards? At least in the old times, people had dignity. Today, people have no self-respect.

Sometimes, even I'm ashamed to call myself a human being. That's why I prefer the company of Theodore over people.

Jane is different; she uses social media to promote her business, and selfies are not included. Her personal Facebook profile security is set on high, so I can't see anything. Her Instagram only has photos of books, but the aesthetic is beautiful and artistic. She writes long captions of what she's up to and what she's reading. I joined her mailing list, and she sends out a newsletter every month. Her Twitter is neglected and her Facebook fan page has a few updates, but the place she's active the most is on Instagram. I study my prey carefully, just as I like to study all of them. I like to see how they lead their lives, what makes them tick. Their habits and quirks. What they like and what they don't like until they become *it*. For now, I'm watching Jane from a distance.

According to her Instagram bio, Jane loves coffee, is obsessed with avocados, but hates cheese. This is not enough. I want more. I want to know what goes on behind the scenes, to learn more about Jane. And to do that, I need access to her phone.

Jane is a woman of routine. All of her days are planned out. A woman of structure and self-discipline, but I guess doing something as challenging as writing books for a living, she needs to be. I suspect she gets little help from her husband, though. Making a living as a writer and to depend solely on that for income is hard as she's not a well-known author. Jane is content: a writer who lives in a nice flat, and although it's not a palace, it's home. It's her nest. Her domain. I'm not sure what her husband does for a living, but I think he is a consultant of some sort. Matthew always carries a laptop with him and it seems he has done well for himself as well. He pays no attention to his car; dirty is an understatement of the state it's in. If a man doesn't bother to wash his car, he's not going to bother about his environment. Jane spends most of the time alone in her flat. When Matthew is home, he locks himself in his office and doesn't come out unless she calls him to eat. Jane loves to cook, and from her Instagram stories, she shares a few photos of her creations. She said a few times cooking is her hobby and by the looks of it, she's amazing at it. How did a woman like Jane end up with a man like Matthew? He's so dull, although they seem happy. Comfortable with one another. By the looks of it, they have been together for a long time. I've seen them plenty of times holding hands when they go for a walk in the neighbourhood, how her eyes have that glow. Her smile reaches her ears, but I do think, however, that deep down, she craves something. Something exciting. Maybe she wonders out of all the men, why on earth she picked this guy? Perhaps because he's the one who can tolerate her. Given she's a writer, she spends a lot of time alone, indoors, jotting down words. It's a solitary job, a writer, like mine. We have a lot of common, her and I. Maybe Jane thought the time was running out and it was time to settle down, or they had been together for so long, they got married because that's the next step in any relationship. I do think she's lonely. I am only assuming all of this, but

I'm looking for a crack; every relationship has one. She's a good woman, doesn't look for trouble. She's loyal, maternal even. From her routine, she upkeeps the flat, cleans and cooks and buys whatever runs out. Washes the clothes and hangs them. Her husband doesn't help out. What more can he want? He has a live-in chef and housekeeper with him.

Chapter Six
Theodore

I stand outside Jane's flat once again. I don't know what Dean has done to her, but it must have frightened her. Why does he have to do this? Go around and cause distress to women? I picture her nestled in her flat, too terrified to go out. Losing her mind with stress and worry. I don't see Matthew, either. Maybe he's in there with her. Neither of them come out. I lie on a car bonnet for hours, waiting, before I walk back to the flat where Dean is on the balcony. He smirks at me; does he know what I'm up to? I'm not a real threat. It's not like I can warn her. Dean wouldn't hurt me. I am the only one in this world he wouldn't hurt, but still, it makes me uneasy. Dean has been going over her phone. It has been a week; would she stay that long without a phone? And why hasn't she had the old phone disconnected yet? I hope she reports this phone and stops him from gaining access into her life. It's scary how people use these apps without realising how much they expose about themselves. She's giving Dean something to feed on. Any piece of information, no matter how small or big, it's progress to him. Dean devours everything. He and I have been in this phase many times before, four times to be exact, but I never saw him as engrossed in anyone as he is with Jane. Maybe Jane has more to offer than the others as Dean had told me they were career women, lawyers, accountants, corporate… not creative like Jane. She is interesting. Different. Special. Maybe he will spare her. If not, I have to find a way to make sure she survives. He's patient and he'll wait. He'll wait as long as it takes; it is all about timing.

A few weeks after the attack, Jane shows her face outside the flat. She's wearing baggy clothes and those funny sunglasses she likes to wear. Jane is clutching something thin in her hand. A phone. What about the old one? She hadn't disconnected it yet. Maybe Jane believes she has lost it and couldn't be bothered. It would be interesting to know how he did it. Little does she know someone has access to it. Jane looks down at me, smiles and keeps on walking. I don't follow her, but I wait. Jane returns a few moments later carrying a shopping bag. Dean is out today. I have no idea where he went, although he doesn't go out during the day; it's in the evenings he goes out the most to meet women or have a drink. The daytime is for work. I call what he does "work" - that's what he calls it too. He's a full-time illustrator, part-time killer. How lovely.

When Dean is working and I go to him so he will play with me, he tells me in a harsh tone, 'Not now, Theodore—can't you see I'm working?'

I know better to leave him alone when he's working and play on my own. It's much more fun that way. I stand on the step of the flat and Jane glances down at me, removing her sunglasses. Her eyes are puffy and red as if she has been crying. She crouches down in front of me and winces as if she's in pain. Did Dean do something to her?

'Hello there again, pudding,' she says.

Jane reaches over hesitantly as if I would bite and strokes my head. In return, I purr and rub my head against her leg.

'What are you doing out here by yourself? Are you lost? You don't look like a stray to me.'

I sit back in front of her proudly. She checks my blue-collar, an uncomfortable thing, but I got used to it. My collar has a tag with my name on it.

'Theodore? How very grown up of you,' she says and pauses. 'Hello, Theodore. I'm Jane.'

I just stare at her.

'You must be someone's precious cat,' she says.

Jane stands back to her level, winces again, and looks around as if she doesn't know what to do with me. I turn and climb the rest of the steps. She glances nervously over her shoulder.

'Oh, what the hell,' she says and opens the lobby door.

Dean had been gone a while and there is a high chance he's on his way. If I don't come home, he'll worry. Jane takes one step at a time with her hand placed on her lower back.

'Oh God, my back is killing me,' she complains.

We walk to the end of the corridor, the keys jingling in her hand.

'I hope you won't get me in trouble,' she continues, unlocking the door.

I take in the flowery scent of the room and rub my body against the chairs to proclaim them as mine. I leap on the sofa and make myself at home. Jane coos and smiles. She puts the kettle on and from the cupboard, she produces a small plate that she fills with water and places by the sofa for me. I ignore it.

'Gosh, I hope the person you live with doesn't think I have taken you for myself.'

I start with my daily grooming session and Jane goes on watching me as if I am doing something remarkable.

'So cute. You look like you dressed for an occasion. A bow tie would look adorable on you.'

She knows her way with cats. Maybe she had one before. I roll on my back to show her I trust her and Jane does not attempt to stroke my belly, which is good. I don't like belly rubs.

'Maybe I should get a cat for myself,' she says.

I stretch on her sofa while she works. I watch her fingers move on the keyboard, which makes me want to play with them. Jane stops sometimes, looks at me, and finds me sitting there watching her. I rub my head against her, marking her, and get a loving stroke for this effort. I purr in response. For a moment, I think of staying here with her, but Dean would go crazy looking for me and I have no reasons to escape. I have a happy home with him. I can't leave him. Not yet, at least. He needs me. I am the only thing in this world that keeps the little humanity he has left. I have to show her that a man wants to cause her harm. Leaving him won't solve anything; it will make matters worse. The intercom screams in the room and we both jump.

Chapter Seven
Dean

Ah, Theodore, my sweet innocent cat. Sometimes I do wonder if he knows what I know. I think he does. Can he sense it? How he constantly watches my every move and follows me in every room. What is he doing in her flat? He had been lingering there a few times. It doesn't bother me; it's not like he's going to confess or anything. By the looks of it, Jane doesn't have too many friends. That is good. The fewer friendships, the better. Fewer people will miss her. Most of her friends are friends of her husband. She goes out for drinks with one of his friend's girlfriends. Her closest friend is a gay man.

Getting her phone is easy. On Friday night, Jane goes out without the husband this time. It seems odd, as they always go out together. She's dressed in a black lace dress and wedge shoes. Jane is more of a trainers sort of girl, rather than the high heels type. I go to see where she's going. She meets a man and after they exchanges kisses, they sit down at the table. The lounge is crowded and I linger by the bar, pretending to be waiting for someone. Her bag is hanging by the chair. I order a drink and wait for the right time. Like most women, she takes her bag with her when she slips into the bathroom. I order another drink. I don't want to have too many; I have to stay focused. The music is so loud, and a crowd gathers by Jane and her friend's table, but they don't seem to notice. I stand and walk past her chair, and her friend is too engrossed talking and making grand gestures with his hands to notice me slipping the bag off the chair. I move along shiftily without taking a backward glance. Purses get lost all the time in places like these and it's not like the security cameras are going to pick anything up, if they're working. I go to the boy's room and walk straight to the cubical. Each time the door opens; house music enters the room, sending vibrations through the bathroom. I open the bag, and inside are her wallet, tobacco and a lighter, a packet of tissues, keys and her phone. I take her phone;

slide it in my pocket and leave. She's still there, and so is the crowd. Jane and her friend are in an intense conversation, their eyes drawn to one another. Jane is holding her wine glass a little too tightly, her knuckles white as if someone is going to take the glass away from her. I walk past her table; would anyone see me? People are gathered together talking and smiling, some dancing. I set the bag on the floor and order myself another drink, acting casual as if nothing happened. A few moments later, she picks up her bag and places it on her lap.

Her phone doesn't have fingerprint nor face recognition. She doesn't believe in high security, our Jane. Cracking the code isn't hard; phones leave fingerprints. All I have to do is take a good look at what numbers have the most tapping and viola. Her Gmail is boring; mostly accounts related to books. Newsletters from book offers. Offers from Asos and other online stores. On her private Facebook account, she only has 120 friends and hardly posts anything on there. She's a member of just two writers' groups, to which she has posted a question or two. Her messages consist of a woman in her fifties named Lisa, another girl who looks hot named Belle, and a writer from Holland, Mary. There are chats with two men; Jack, the one she was having drinks with. The other is Edward. I look at their profiles. Jack is a makeup artist who owns a salon not far from here. Edward shares his Facebook profile with his partner Caleb. Some people get joint bank accounts, others get joint Facebook accounts. There are a few messages from her husband. The last message she sent him is her telling him to take out the rubbish. Usual household duties. Her activities have been quiet. What I have access to is her Dropbox, where all of her manuscripts are saved. I read those without touching anything as it alerts its users. There are early drafts and unfinished manuscripts. She writes a lot, but this is what she does for a living. As I suspect, she gets little help from her husband. There is no way she can live comfortably from just from her writing.

The day after I took her phone, it beeped with a Facebook message. It was her messaging Edward on her laptop.

Jane: I have lost my phone 😞 *I don't know how this could have happened. I'm always so careful.*

Edward: Oh no, Jane, did you report it stolen?

Jane: No, it's no big deal. Phones get stolen all the time. It's not like the police will go and look for it.

Edward: Oh, come on, Jane I know the police won't look for it but at least have it shut down. You wouldn't know in what kind of hands that phone got into. For a crime author, you are so sloppy.

Jane: It's password protected.

Edward: And it's so hard to crack the code!

Jane: Ok, I'm not being completely honest but Matthew got us this new plan on our phones and he's paying the bill, so I don't want him to know I've lost it. We have been arguing a lot lately and I want to keep the peace. I'll just replace the phone and go to the company myself and have it all arranged without him knowing.

Edward: How is Matthew?

Jane: He's busy always working and I'm always working, so it's taking its toll on both of us, and the last thing I want is to tell him I lost my phone.

Edward: So you haven't got the new phone, and don't you think he'll find out you have no phone?'

Jane: In all honesty, Ed, I doubt he would notice, but I'm going today to have it replaced.

Edward: Ah, Jane, I love you but you are such a baby sometimes. You and Matthew should go on a weekend getaway to ease the stress.

Jane: Money is tight at the moment. See you soon xxx

But Jane doesn't go out and get the new phone like she promised she would. I know because I'm keeping my eye out. She stays locked in that flat, writing, I would guess. I have Matthew to thank for picking up the phone bill; I was getting worried she might shut it down, but now that she doesn't want to show him that she has lost it because it would result in them fighting, I'm granted access. They are fighting, she said. I wonder about that. She also said money is tight. I bet they argue about money; that's what most couples fight about. That's what most of the arguments me and my ex-wife had. I noticed Theodore isn't home. He usually comes back at 4:00 pm from his walk. I always find him on the sofa waiting for me. I look for him under the kitchen table, under the sofa, and I even take a few treats to trick him into coming out from wherever he's hiding, but nothing. I make myself a cup of coffee, my brain ticking like a time bomb. What if he's run over by a car? What if he escaped? What if someone stole him? I would kill anyone who dared to steal my beloved cat. He's the centre of my universe. My everything. I lean against the kitchen counter, sipping on my coffee. I go out to the balcony and I find myself staring at her apartment. The curtains are closed, and then it clicks. Would he? But Theodore doesn't like anyone, and he's not that trusting either. The bugger… what is he up to?

Chapter Eight
Theodore

Jane sighs, places the laptop on the coffee table, walks to the intercom, and squints at the small screen. She looks at me, then frowns and presses a button.

'Yes?'

I stand to attention. *Oh no, no, no.* How did he figure out I'm here? I didn't go out to the balcony, so he couldn't have seen me. I have overstayed my welcome, and I'm usually home at this hour. He must have returned home, didn't find me and got worried. What have I done? Jane and Dean shouldn't meet.

'Yes, he's here,' she says, and presses a button.

No! They shouldn't be introduced! This shouldn't happen. I want to form a friendship with her without him knowing about it.

She cringes while passing a long glance at me. The lock makes a loud *clunk*, and I sit up straight and tilt my head sideways.

'You have been found,' she whispers to me as she opens the door.

'I'm sorry, I don't want you to think I've stolen him… I found him outside, he followed me and…' She places her hand on her cheek and red splotches appear on her neck. I'm not sure if she's embarrassed about the whole situation or if it's because of him. Maybe both. I jump off the sofa and walk to the door, meowing. Dean glances down at me, his eyes wide. Jane is silently gazing at him in a dazzled sort of way.

'It's quite all right,' he says. 'Thank you for taking care of him.'

'It's my pleasure. He's a very beautiful cat,' she says.

She's blushing uncontrollably. 'Err… I'm Jane. You must live around here given…' She trails off, touching her ear.

'Yes, I live right across the street. I'm Dean.'

I meow and he picks me up. 'I'd better be on my way…' he adds. 'Thanks again for looking after him.'

'Y-yes… of course, anytime. B-bye.'

Humans are so awkward.

Dean walks away stroking my head. 'What were you thinking going to her like that?'

When we get home, he puts me down and slides the balcony door closed.

'You are not supposed to go there. She's not supposed to know we exist. At least *me*,' he says. 'Not for now, at least.'

His voice is calm and soothing. I don't know which is worse: him being angry or him being like this. What does he mean not for now? He has a plan to get close to her. Why?

'Don't go there,' he says as if I'm a human and I understand what he means. 'But of course, you'll go there again. You have no idea what I'm saying. Yet I still talk to you as if you are a human. You're the only friend I have, you know that?'

A week goes by and Dean doesn't open the balcony door for me. Nor let me go out. I misbehaved and this is his way to punish me, but he knows punishments do not work on me. I have to be careful not to undermine him, though. Jane knows about him now and that is a problem. He looks at me with wryness and he says I'm his companion. There was a brief interaction with Jane, but he wants more of her. He goes on tracking her phone. He's like a vampire sucking information. Nobody would suspect the handsome man; why would they? I wish she blocked her phone. But that gives me another wave of despair – what would he do if she blocks that phone? How far is Dean willing to go until he eliminates her? I wonder how he'd do it. Would it be a trip down the stairs? The window? A car accident? A fire? The possibilities are endless.

Jane and Matthew have a good stable relationship and knowing Dean is going to destroy it fills me with disquietude.

'So... now it all makes sense,' Dean says scrolling through the phone. 'No wonder she's always at home. No wonder they are arguing and money is tight.' He goes on. I look at him. Dean has found something, a solution to tear Jane and Matthew's world apart. He looks at me and strokes my head. 'Guess what, Theodore... I found something. Her husband suffers from depression,' he says and stands from the sofa. I stare at him.

'Ah, never mind...' he says and goes back to the phone.

Reading those chats gives Dean a motive, a way out for her. He goes to the window.

'You'll never feel under-appreciated ever again,' he says. 'Not while I'm around.'

Desperation seizes me. I meow and meow, but Dean doesn't budge.

'What is it Theodore? You want to play?' he asks. 'Here.'

He fetches my ball. I watch the blue plastic slide on the floor but I ignore it. Dean sighs and turns back to the window. I know what he's going to do. He is going to kill her husband. Why, though? It's her he wants, not her husband – what will he gain by killing him? What is he thinking? He moves away from the window and goes to the kitchen, puts the kettle on and opens the drawer under the stove. He produces a small bottle and places it on the countertop. The kettle whistles and he takes it off the stove to make himself a cup of coffee. I'm sitting on the sofa with my head tilted to one side. He smiles and opens another cupboard.

'You don't want play, so I suppose you want this...' Dean tells me, his head hidden behind the cupboard.

The squashing of a packet indicates it's treat time, but even that doesn't wash away my trepidation. Dean picks me up and places me on his lap. He's holding the stick between his thumb and index finger, waiting for me to take it from him as he trained me to do, but I jump off the sofa. He frowns.

'What is it with you today?' he pleads.

I climb on the granite countertop and smell the bottle. It's made of glass. I can't smell anything apart from Dean's scent, but I have seen this bottle before. *Succinylcholine*.

Chapter Nine
Theodore

The flashing of lights captures my attention. The ambulance cries in the distance at first, but it approaches closer and closer to the street. My ears prickle with the sounds: a car door slamming, footsteps and voices. Dean is on the bed, but he's not asleep. He's wide awake with a hand on his forehead as if he has a fever. A few hours before, Dean left the flat, taking the *Succinylcholine* with him.

He fed me when he arrived, but Dean was silent and didn't say a word to me. He's normally cheery when he sees me as if we have been apart for a long time. His eyes are hidden behind his long lashes. I know this behaviour too well, but I don't want to think about it. He went to have a shower, laid on the bed and never got up. Now, it's like he's sleeping with his eyes open. I hop off the bed and go to the window. There is an ambulance and police cars, and people scattering in the street like poker cards.

Others are looking down from their balconies. I meow to get Dean's attention, but he won't move. I climb off the window and go to the bed to lie by his feet.

Dean had killed, and when he kills, he becomes unaidable, as if he mourns for the victim. Maybe he has a hard time believing he's capable of taking a life. To cause that amount of pain to someone else.

He feeds me, but ignores me. Doesn't play with me. He doesn't turn on the laptop to work. He just stays like that, hashed. This goes on for a day or two, then he starts to talk, and when he does, his voice is soothing and low, like a whisper.

'When you kill so much, you become hollow and empty,' he tells me, stroking the spot behind my ear.

He likes to talk to me about his killings. About things I simply do not understand. It helps him, having me to talk to, and the fact I can't run for help makes it all the better for him.

'It becomes a habit, killing,' he says. 'You do it again and again and you don't blink. Of course, the first time, I cried and I hated myself. I went to the police station to report the crime,' he confesses.

The TV is turned on to a crime show, and a can of beer is on the coffee table.

'But I couldn't make myself go in.'

He looks down at me, and I gaze up at him.

'You have no idea what I'm saying, do you?' he asks.

It's evident Dean had gone and done it. He has killed Jane's husband, and now I'm very curious to know how; the one thing I know is it involved the *Succinylcholine*.

To Dean, Matthew was a problem and had to be eliminated. Dean thinks that Matthew was the weak link and caused Jane stress. She had to take care of him when it should be the other way around. Matthew was the one who was supposed to take care of her. Matthew didn't treat her right. All she did was cook, clean like a maid and babysit him while he locked himself in his office and didn't come out unless it was necessary. I disagree. Dean had taken him away from her. Jane would never see him again, hold him or see his face. Jane thought she would never be alone, but now she is. I don't want to imagine what she's feeling, how distraught she must be. To take someone so important from someone else's life... it's like Dean decided for her. I'm ashamed of my human. Who is he to dictate if Matthew wasn't good enough? She's the one who knows that, not Dean. Jane married the guy; she knew what she was doing and what she signed up for. What is Dean going to do? Go after her loved ones and kill them one by one? Would he take Matthew's stead? But Matthew can never be replaced. He'd remain in her heart forever. I saw her today; someone, a loved one, I suppose, came to pick her up. She wore sunglasses and baggy clothes. Her face was devoid of colour. Jane didn't come home that evening, or the one after, or the next. A day ago, according to what Dean had read aloud, Jane posted on all of her social media accounts that she'd be going on a hiatus.

Jane doesn't leave any clues to what she's up to or where she is. She must have had disconnected the apps from her phone. Dean finally lets me out, and I go for a leisurely walk under the sun. Two neighbours gather nearby: one is sweeping the step, and the other has a grocery bag in her hand. It all looks serene. The sun is out, but the weather is getting cooler now. On the island, it takes a while for the cold to set in. The lady with the groceries glances down at me and smiles. They talk about trivial things, (what they cooked for supper, the weather, how the prices went up), and then the subject shifts.

'Have you seen her?'

'No… such a tragedy, suicide.'

Suicide. Dean covered the murder by making it look as if her husband had killed himself. Of course he would do that. Dean is not your average killer; he's imperceptible. It had to be believable, something that couldn't be traced to him.

'I know. The poor thing. He should have asked for help not gone and taken his own life like that. Locking himself in the garage and leaving the engine running, blocking the exhaust pipe so he would asphyxiate…'

Asphyxiate? It sounds lethal. Dean had used *Succinylcholine*. I don't know what effect the *Succinylcholine* has, but knowing Dean, it would be something undetectable. It makes sense, of course. Dean likes to learn about other people's weaknesses and make them work in his favour. I go back home, thinking of how sad the whole situation is. For a moment, I think of running away and becoming a stray. I'm carrying a large burden. My human has too many dark secrets. Too many demons. Tonight, Dean has gone out. I can play with my toys, but I don't feel like it. So I stay in the bed in the dark, wide awake, waiting. I wait for a long time until the front door opens, and I leap off the bed. There are deep inhales of breath. Dean has brought company, a lady. He has her hands pinned on the wall and is kissing her. I hide under the table, not interested, not wanting to know. I tuck my tail under me, feeling cosy in my happy place, in my little corner, while my ears can't help but move with each sound. Shoes are taken off, zippers, the woman is practically screaming.

In the morning, I wait for Dean to get up and feed me, but he hasn't awoken yet. So, I wait. The bedroom door is locked, but murmurs are coming from behind it. I don't know why humans close doors. I don't know why they have doors in the first place. Sometimes when he closes the door, I wonder if Dean would ever come out. Would he feed me again? What happens if he never comes out of that door? I climb on the furniture and the door opens, and a woman with straight black hair comes out. The woman is petite and has long nails that I think are painted. Dean leaves the room shirtless walking her to the door. The woman gives him a sloppy kiss on the lips and leaves, telling him what a great night she had and thanked him for it. They exchange phone numbers. After she leaves, Dean sighs and turns to spot me sitting there, judging him.

'What are you looking at?' he says before shutting the bedroom door.

Chapter Nine
Dean

Jane chats with Mary and in a recent conversation with her, Jane told Mary about Matthew and his history with depression. Jane says it stresses her out to constantly worry, to wake up with apprehension, wondering if he'd be good today. Sometimes she writes that she wishes to turn her back on everything, run away, and be free from it all. She feels it every day, the weight burying her, to look after him and the upkeep of the apartment. Every day, she feels like she's growing older and older.

I'm an old woman at thirty-three. It is so hard to be strong all the time when all I want to do is scream. I sound like a bitch for saying this, but I don't feel appreciated.

Her husband always parked the car in the garage. There are no cameras installed, so that's good news. *Succinylcholine* is a powerful muscle relaxer, if you can call it that, more like putting the body into a paralysing state. It was used in surgeries, but the effect doesn't last very long. As I said, my mum was a doctor. I never cared much for what she did. Yes, my mum was doctor and it is one of the most important professions, helping people, saving lives, but to me, it's a job just the same. It put food on the table, allowed us to live comfortably, pay the bills, and paid for my brother's and me studies. I am grateful for my mum's hard work. If it weren't for her job, we would have been buried in tuition fees. But what never fails to amaze me is how we are constantly judged by what we do. A doctor is looked up to; people respect them, while a janitor is looked down upon. You're not good enough. A job gives you an identity as if it defines you. To me what my mum did was just a job that paid well and people fussed. In the end, she was still our mum.

'You must be so proud your mum being a doctor,' I had been told. Or 'You can't fake being sick with your old lady being a doctor.' Bla, bla, bla. Her being a doctor didn't stop what I have become but it's not her fault she gave birth to a bad seed.

I dropped by to help her move some things down to the garage one afternoon as she was getting rid of junk in the house. We don't have junk lying about where we lived, which is a nice cottage, always kept pristine. She likes to clear up a lot and buy new items to replace the old ones. She takes pride in it while my dad sits in front of TV reading the paper, not paying attention to her latest project.

'Take this as well, dear,' she said, pointing at a white medicine chest.

'But you might need this,' I said.

She gave me a slight wave of the hand. 'If I need it, I'll go down there for it.'

I lifted the chest and carried it down to the garage. There was a paddle of oil on the ground from my dad's old 1972 Ford Cortina that he refuses to sell. It is a beautiful piece of machinery if he would only restore a little. It had a flat tyre, and I suppose it's still that way. The seats need to be changed, the body needs work, and the colour, a dark green, needs a good touch up.

I was on my feet, and the next thing I knew, I was facing the ceiling after slipping on the leak. I wasn't hurt, but the chest was face down and opened. I cursed and started to pick at the pills, bandages and surgical gloves when I saw a small glass bottle. I was surprised it didn't break. The label read *Succinylcholine*. I don't know why she had it in the house or what she used it for, so I did a quick Google search. I could have asked her, but I felt more secure Googling it. I found what I was looking for and pocketed it. If Mum asked where it was, I could say it must have gotten lost when I dropped the chest.

Matthew has gone out, so has Jane, who went to meet her friend for a drink. When Matthew comes back an hour later, I go down to the garage. The door is wide open and I hide in a darkened corner, putting on my leather gloves. As I hear him closing the door, I move slowly. Blood pumps in my veins with the anticipation of what's to come. My heart rockets against my chest and for a moment, I thought he could hear it too. He has his back to me and I see he has earbuds in. When he feels the sting of the needle, he turns to react. One of the earbuds drops from his ear, and I hear a man talking. For a moment, I think he's on the phone. He pushes me and attempts to punch me, which I dodge. He comes after me, tries to say something, but nothing comes out. The chemical has already worked into his system. His eyes are wide and this is the best part: when they start to lose control of their own body. Sweat breaks out on his temples as his eyes become consumed with fear while trying to get a sense of what's happening. His legs go limp and he drops to his knees. His hands tumble under him and he falls flat on his face. I take the bunch of keys from the floor and close the door to the garage. I place him on the driver's seat, then block the silencer and start the engine. I inject another dose just to be sure. It is all too easy and so clean.

Who would find him? Not Jane since she's out. Or maybe when she gets home, she won't find him there and will call him, but he won't pick up, then she'll get worried and go the in the garage to check. It doesn't matter now.

Jane is making it impossible for me to track her as she's no longer active on any of her social media accounts. She's in mourning. I have trouble understanding why people say bad things about their loved ones. Like wanting to run away from them or while being with them, they wish they were elsewhere. Then, the husband dies and it's a river of tears. Hypocrisy at its best.

When someone dies, no matter how terrible that person was when they were alive, they're praised. Why is that? Because everyone loves you when you're dead. Don't speak ill of the dead. It's how it is and how it will remain.

Jane will get over it in time. She'll move on because that's what life is all about, paddling along.

Jane is in hiding, but I'm not worried; she will come back. I presume she's with her family.

Maybe I have gone too far this time. Perhaps it was wrong to pick her, a woman who has commitments. *Had*. She has one less burden to worry about. I did her a favour; she's a wife, not a bloody carer. She's a woman who takes her vows seriously, and I like that about her. Jane is loyal. Now she's free and open to the world, thanks to me.

The urge to kill doesn't come all the time - it comes and goes. When it does, it claws at me. I've had girlfriends, but I had no desire to hurt them. I never wanted to hurt Carol and there were times she made me angry. Anger, however, is an emotion that makes you impulsive, and I tried to keep the fury at bay. Anger is not the most powerful emotion; fear is.

I enjoy the company of women. I find them to be stimulating and sensual. I love sex and I enjoy having sex with them. After I kill, I shut off. I never understand why I do this. Theodore watches my every move, always studying me, always observing me, always on alert. I bet this cat can read me. I wonder what he really thinks of me, but when I look at him, all I see is a beautiful creature with no worries, content in his world, peaceful and innocent. And mankind is the civilised kind? Such bullshit.

I go out in the evening for a drink, to reflect on nothing in particular. It's all part of my routine after I kill. It's a way to celebrate the victim's life in a fucked-up way. Because I killed Jane's husband, it doesn't mean I won't have a drink for his life. The air is getting cooler now. The wind whistles in the trees and music of the band playing trumpets echoes somewhere nearby. There must be one of the village's feasts they do here, one of the last ones of the summer. This is what I like about this island; they celebrate everything. The streets are decorated with the red and gold tapestries. These preparations take a long time, but the churches are lit up and the statue of the Saint who that church is dedicated to is paraded down the streets where people would join in. There are food trucks and music. It's lovely, but tonight I'm not in the mood.

It's Wednesday and its ladies' night, which means a discount for them. I glance at those young girls with their hair extensions, fake nails and fake eyelashes. Wearing too much makeup to impress the next arsehole, trying to look pretty when a little less would make them look better. A girl who's probably in her late teens, early twenties, is checking me out and says something to her friends. They all look in my direction to make it more obvious she's talking about me. They giggle and start to snap selfies to upload to Instagram or Facebook to seek the approval from those strangers, looking for compliments about how fabulous and great they are. But all they're displaying is how low their self-esteem is.

A woman comes in and sits on the stool next to me. She orders a drink with the barman, continuing to tap on her phone before she huffs and slams the phone down. I can guess what the scenario is here: she planned to meet some guy and he bailed on her. She has blonde hair and lips that are a bit too plump. She's attractive in a seductive sort of way.

'Are you alone?' she asks in a thick accent. Eastern European by the sounds of it.

'Yep.'

'Do you often drink by yourself?' she asks.

'No.'

We talk about trivial things, the weather, about living here, what we do for a living. The same old conversation. The girl from earlier is looking in my direction with disappointment on her face.

The woman stands from her stool. 'I have to go.'

I lift my glass at her in salute.

I finish my drink and turn to look at the girl who's talking to her friends, but our eyes meet. This is all a game to me. I can have this girl so easily and since I'm lonely and in a shitty mood, I play along and take this girl along for the ride to kill time. To feel a little better about myself. Theodore is enough in some nights, but not in all of them. He would curl on top of me while I lay in bed, feeling his warmth, while he purrs and looks at me with those huge eyes. Tonight, he won't do. I stand and walk up to her and her eyes grow large as I approach. The score is already set; this girl would go anywhere with me. I say hello and she turns into the colour of a beetroot as she mutters her hello. Her friends are looking at us, probably jealous that she set her eyes on a guy and now she's about to have him. The girl has my full-undivided attention, so her friends won't matter for the time being. It's just me and her. She introduces herself as Hollie and I offer her a drink, which she accepts. I take her away from her friends as they watch us with their mouths hanging open. The girl looks at me as if she hit the jackpot and despite my misgivings, I feel generous. I ask her the basic questions, the same old same old. She's twenty-two years old, works in a nail salon. We talk, but all the while, all I can think about is taking her home and fucking her. I will take her home and I *will* fuck her. After an hour, I tell her I'm leaving and she looks sad, but I give her a light kiss on the lips.

'Can I see you again?' she asks.

'Would you like to come with me?'

'Where?' she asks stupidly as if she doesn't know what I'm referring to.

I'm not going to beat around the bush; I'll be direct. Woman are supposed to like honest men.

'To my place.'

'Well.. err... I barely know you.'

'Isn't that how it starts?' I ask huskily.

She huffs and walks away to inform her friends. I know what they're probably saying: *going where with him? No, you don't know him. Don't you think he's a bit too old for you?* That I could be dangerous and a serial killer. I am both, but there will be no killing tonight, not with her friends glued to their phones, possibly tracking her location and sending her messages. It's becoming rather impossible to commit a crime these days. I don't kill in my home and not with Theodore there. He's too pure to be exposed to such violence. Apart from that, she doesn't fit the criteria. When Hollie comes home with me, I don't waste either her or my time. She submits to me as I take her by the door with her legs wrapped around me. Killing and sex are the two things that are real. One is the creation of life, the other is the end of it. They go hand in hand.

Chapter Ten
Theodore

I'm on the balcony hunting a fly when a car pulls up to the curb and Jane comes out of it. I walk to the railing to take a closer look. Tiny droplets of rain dot her sunglasses. She looks smaller, as if she has shrunk after Matthew's death. *Murder.* Jane keeps her head low as she carries two bags with her. Dean comes out with a bottle of beer in one hand and one of my ball toys in the other while Jane fiddles with the lobby door to fit the key in. He takes this in and the fear looms over me as his lips curl into a tight smile. Jane's body is slack as if she gave up, or got fed up or both. The door opens and a middle-age woman comes out. They chat for a while, then go their separate ways. Dean throws the ball across the room and I chase after it. He leans his shoulder against the balcony door as he watches me moving the ball with my paw while taking sips of his beer.

'That's is a good boy,' he says.

Three days after her arrival, Jane comes out of the flat and returns fifteen minutes later. I wait for her by the step of the flat. When she returns from her errand, she smiles thinly at me as if she's lost all motivation to do anything. I meow in greeting. She gives me a few strokes. I rub my body against her and meow again.

'Hello, Theodore. So lovely to see you again.'

I follow her inside and I keep my tail straight to show her how happy I am that I get to spend time with her. Jane fumbles in her handbag for the keys and opens the door. Dropping her bags on the floor, Jane heads straight to the sofa and lies down, burying her face in the cushion. I look out onto the balcony, then climb on the sofa and lie next to her. Tears fall down her cheeks. I purr as if this might offer her comfort, as if it will take all her pain away and bring him back.

I want to stay there, tucked under the safety of her small flat.

'My husband killed himself,' she says in a small voice. 'I'm all alone. I don't think I can live without him, to face the days knowing I'll never see him again. Not be able to talk to him again. I miss him so much. Why did he have to take his own life? I'm going over on my head trying to see the signs. Looking for warnings. What I might have missed. I'm trying to understand why he would do that. It's so selfish of him. We had our problems. No marriage is perfect, but we were happy. I thought he *was* happy. Why did he leave me behind? He was the light that guided me home; now, that light is gone and all there is, is darkness.'

If only you knew what I know, Jane, I want to tell her. Your husband had no intention of killing himself and leaving you behind. You're in so much pain because someone else took your husband away and covered it up to make it look like he had taken his own life. My human killed your husband and he's coming after you if I don't do something about it.

Jane wipes the tears away. 'I'm too young to be a widow, but life doesn't prepare you for these things. Nothing does. It comes when it comes,' she says, standing.

'Do you cats mourn? Do you care?' she asks me.

I stare at her. We do, yes. Maybe we take less time than dogs, but we do.

How on Earth am I going to stop Dean from killing Jane? How could I warn her? Never in my life have I ever felt so helpless.

When the buzzer sounds, I know it's Dean. Jane rubs her eyes with her hands and stands there for a while as the persistent buzzing pierces the apartment and she motions to the door. I walk along with her as Dean stands before us. He looks down at me with disapproval before he picks me up.

'I'm sorry...' he says apologetically. 'He keeps bothering you. I don't know what's gotten into him.'

'It's quite alright—he's a wonderful distraction...' She pauses and shuts her eyes. 'He's good company.'

'I'm very sorry,' he says, 'for your loss.'

Look at him offering her sympathies when he's responsible for this. How could he? How could he just stand there and say that to her?

'Thank you,' Jane says.

He strokes my coat and looks at me, then at her, then to me again. I push my ears backwards and my eyes are wide. What he's going to do now?

'Would you like to keep him for a few days? It's clear he likes you.'

'Um… you want me to keep your cat?' she asks incredulously.

'Sure. I think it will help with…' he trails off.

'I'll think about it, but thanks for the offer,' she says and shuts the door.

Have me for a few days? What am I, a trophy? Dean is what he is, but he's my human; we share a bond. This has to be part of his scheme, but the fact that he's using me, an innocent cat, for his twisted agenda, using me as bait, doesn't sit well with me.

Chapter Eleven
Dean

For an unknown reason, I compare my younger self to Hollie, although we come from different spectrums. When I was her age, social media was only starting and I had already killed two women. And met Carol. Relationships are tiresome and complicated, but I don't mind the commitment. I loved the comfort and the warmth it provided at least; I try to feel those things as much as I can. Hollie is sweet, but annoying and immature. She ignores Theodore, pretends he's not there, and I don't like that. My cat is part of me; he's part of my life, but to her, he blends in like he's part of the sofa. A stuffed toy. Not real. Doesn't she know men who own cats are meant to be smart, clean and never boring? She's not interested in me, per se, but what I can offer her. What I can give her. I'm thirty years old; in her eyes, I'm experienced. A man, not a boy. I don't play games as boys do. I know how to please her and I'm willing to do so. I don't mind. She comes over, tapping on her phone and the Facebook messenger doesn't stop binging.

'Would you like something to drink?' I ask.

She stays glued to her phone. 'Coke if you have it.'

'Sorry. I don't.'

She proceeds with the tapping, not paying attention to me. Annoyance sends an electric pulse into me, and I clutch my hands into fists.

'Hollie, did you hear me?' I say, keeping my tone measured.

'What? Sorry,' she says, not sounding sorry at all.

I stare at her. 'I just told you I don't have coke.'

'Oh, I'll have whatever.'

'I'm afraid I don't have that either,' I reply.

Can't she just lose the phone for a few hours? The phone bings again and she jumps to it. Jesus Christ!

'Water,' she says.

I pour her a glass of water. She settles on the sofa; her nails are long painted in a neon green that hurts my eyes. How is she able to type with her nails that long? I get that she works in a nail salon, but is having her nails like knives really necessary?

I hand her a glass of water. I stay like this for a while, with the glass between us. The irritation is bubbling now. I watch her coldly as music comes from her phone. Now what? She looks up and takes the glass without saying thank you. I'm starting to feel insignificant. I adjust my life to meet hers, can't she do the same?

'What are you doing?' I ask.

'I'm on *Tik Tok*.'

'On what?'

Now I have her full attention, Hollie is looking at me as if I have been hiding under a rock all this time. I keep my expression passive so she won't read into my coldness, but now I am offended that she's looking at me like this. Does she know what I could do to her? How easily I could terminate her pathetic existence? No, of course not; all she sees is my exterior, the hot English guy with great hair.

'You know Instagram, right?' she says.

Is that arrogance in her tone?

'Yeah, I've heard of it,' I say.

'Well, it's like Instagram but it's for videos,' she purrs.

'How lovely,' I say sarcastically.

'I know right?' she says with enthusiasm, showing me her phone. "Look." I look at the screen, where there are two girls dancing to a song on the stairs.

'Hmm, very interesting,' I say.

She doesn't read into this piece of sarcasm either. She's not fluent in it. Most people aren't. She lifts her phone to face her and adjusts her hair. I swear my heart stops for a moment. Is she doing what I think she's doing? For God's sake, over my dead body.

'This is a photo-free zone,' I say as calmly as I can allow, even though I want to grab that phone and throw it out into the street.

She blinks at me as if this is unheard of.

'Don't take selfies.' I say so she understands.

Now she looks hurt. I look away so she doesn't see me roll my eyes.

'You can't be serious. I thought we could take one together.'

'Why?'

'Well look at me and look at you and my followers will wonder who the stud is. Besides that's what people do,' she reasons as if this is a law and it needs to be implemented by force. As if people don't have a choice not to share their life with the rest of the world.

Young people today don't know how to appreciate other people's privacy. Everything needs an audience. I sit next to her and put my arm around her.

'I feel like I'm sharing you with that thing. Why don't you put it away and we can enjoy each other instead,' I offer.

She melts into me as her sticky glossed lips press against mine. I lie her down on the sofa and plant kisses on her neck. My hand goes under her skirt as if a treasure chest lay under there. The phone is long forgotten and I thank God for this face that hides what lies beneath.

Jane is back; it's about time she would crawl back from whatever rock she was hiding under. It must be so hard for her to live in a place she shared with her husband. All those memories. To sleep in the bed where she once had slept with him and now, she wakes up to find it empty. To not hear him type on his computer. To not have him sit next to her while having dinner. Not cooking for him or cleaning up after him. I had been responsible for that. Jane is burdened by this pain because of me. Jane mourns because of me. Jane moves on because of me. Jane will be free because of me. She's back online gradually, starting to build on what she left off. Soon, everything will return to normal. She chats with Jack. I always read these texts after she has finished chatting to risk having that annoying "seen."

Jane: *Something weird happened today.*
Jack: *Really, what?*

Jane: A cat of a neighbour keeps coming to my door. I feel sorry for the little guy and I let him in. Twice, his owner had to come and collect the poor fellow. The other day, his owner asked me if I'd like to have his cat for a few days.

Jack: What do you mean?

Jane: You know, to help with what happened. For company.

Jack: You can always adopt a cat.

Jane: My point exactly, and there is another problem.

Jack: What?

Jane: The guy. He's gorgeous. I mean a sight to behold sort of gorgeous.

Jack: Send me a pic.

Jane: Wait, let me go and knock on his door and ask for a selfie. 😂

Jack: What's his name?

Jane: Dean.

Jack: So, him being good looking is a problem?

Jane: Why would he ask me to have his cat to stay with me?

Jack: I don't know… To get inside your pants, perhaps.

Jane: There is no way a man that stunning would be interested in a widowed blob of potato like me. I must look like a can of baked beans compared to the women he dates. Oh, maybe he's married. I don't know.

Edward: Jane, stop it. You're going through some life-changing moments and it's tough, but you're an attractive can of baked beans. You didn't check for a ring?

Jane: Checking if attractive males wear wedding rings is the last thing on my mind right now. Most men don't wear them either.

Jack: And you're talking about this alleged attractive man. You have two options: either you are going to take him up on the offer or not. Got to go, sweet cheeks. Speak to you soon xxx.

Edward sends her a message just as I'm about to put the phone away. I let them chat for a while until it goes silent.

Edward: How are you?

Jane: Coping, but it's hard. I miss him. I was thinking the other day how I wasted so much time on pointless things arguing about stupid stuff and now I will never argue or fight with him again.

Edward: 🙁

Jane: *At least he's at peace now.*

Edward: *This is all too shocking and so sad. But I do hope he's at peace too. Did you solve the issue with the old phone? I always meant to ask but forgot. A lot has happened.*

Jane: *No, but working on it. I'm going tomorrow.*

Edward: *Jane, I thought you said you'd take care of it months ago. Block it! And do a fingerprint and face recognition on your new phone.*

Jane: *I know, I know. I'm not good when it comes to these things. There is so much to do, paperwork and stuff.*

Edward: *I could do it for you but they would need your details and signature.*

Jane: *I'm on it tomorrow. Oh God, it feels like big brother with this face recognition crap. I miss the old days when everything was simple. A phone call did the trick, not being reachable all the time.*

Edward: *It's for security.*

Jane: *I'll get on with it. Xx.*

I can wave this phone goodbye if she's shutting it down tomorrow. If she does, I already have another plan.

After I killed Ann, I had nightmares of her twisted body on the floor. I didn't kill again soon; the urge stopped, and I went on with my life, thinking that everything was normal. This, however, was like I popped open a bottle of champagne, only the cork wasn't going back into the bottle. If I got away with it once, would I be able to get away with it the second time? I was studying art in uni when I found the next one. Her name was Jamie. She was a plain girl, not popular.

Picking a popular person is a fatal mistake; too many things can go wrong. She took the same classes as me and always sat at the back. We never interacted, but I watched her, learning about her movements. Her routine was predictable: from home to uni, back and forth. She didn't go out and kept herself to herself. Eventually, Jamie did nothing in particular. No boyfriends either. She might have been a virgin. I got bored easily with her. That urge to kill her was eating at me, not letting me sleep, not leaving me alone. I had to stop it. So after uni one afternoon, I went to the street she always took to her apartment and waited in a corner. My heart thundered in my chest. I didn't have to do it. I had a chance to turn away and forget about it and go seek help. Sweat gathered on my temples. I checked my watch… any minute now. No, I thought, I felt like shit when I killed Ann. I had gone to the police station to turn myself in. I peeked from the wall and she was coming; she had earbuds in, oblivious, possibly daydreaming. My heart rocketed. I glanced away, staring ahead under the hood I was wearing, and shut my eyes as my back grew moist with sweat. I opened my eyes; the bus drove past. Jamie walked with her backpack slung across her shoulder. The red bus stopped at the curb, and as Jamie crossed the road, I let that monster eat me. For weeks on end, I tried to spare her. I don't have to be like this. I don't have to be this person. I argued silently with myself. *But you are this person. You killed before and you'll do it again. Think of the power it gave you, the control. You can feel like God for a few minutes.* That violent, angry monster seethed at me. It hissed, making my head hurt. *It's not like she's important. She's a loser and you'd do her an enormous favour.* To shut this voice up, I tried to keep myself occupied. Drawing ended up with me drawing dead girls, so that was no good. Instead, I went out with my mates, partied for a bit and had a few one-night stands. But two weeks later, I saw her again in class. I watched how she was always yawning during this lecture. The rain dotted windows and a thunder roared in the sky. After class, I followed her through the corridor, but walked past her and left the building. Outside, the rain poured heavily, but I had no umbrella with me, so I pulled the hood of my jacket up and walked on. The thunder pulsed in the sky. The air smelled of rain, crisp and fresh. I found myself waiting in the same corner, leaning against the wall. I took a peek out to the street as the rain slowed slightly. My chest was heavy and my heart raced. She was walking towards me with a red umbrella and earbuds. The bus was a few metres behind her at the red light, and I placed my foot on the corner so it poked out. I heard her approach and she tripped on my foot. The umbrella slipped from her hand and she was in the middle of the road. I moved to the alley with my hood still over my head. All I heard was a distinct sound like a *pop* when the body hit the vehicle and someone screaming. The case did make it to the news: a woman tripped and fell into an upcoming bus. It was about being at the wrong place at the wrong time.

Chapter Twelve
Theodore

Hollie comes over to the flat, and I don't know what Dean is doing with her. Maybe for company or to have someone to mate with. One afternoon, while Dean is in the bathroom and Hollie is on the sofa scrolling through her phone, I stretch on the sofa, arch my back, yawn and sit down. I tilt my head sideways at Hollie and her mouth curls, not in delight, but with a look of utter disgust. What is her problem anyway?

'You're gross,' she tells me. 'You look like a rat with a cuter outfit.'

How dare she? Does she know the difference between my kind and rodents? Is Hollie aware she just compared me to my prey?

It doesn't take Jane long to think about it. Not long at all. She's behind the door.

'Hi, um… I was wondering if the offer of me adopting Theodore for a few days still stands?' she asks.

'Of course. Please, come in.' he says.

I don't mind going home with her, but it means a change of an environment for me. I'm not acquainted with her place apart from the living room. Cats are territorial creatures and unfamiliar places can cause us anxiety and stress. Dean is willing to put me through that and more to get to his end goal. He's more curious about Jane as a person rather than a subject that he would kill. Hollie is due to come over, so I'm glad I'll be at Jane's. I don't want to listen to any of her nonsense and she doesn't like me. It's a good thing I'll be out of the way. Dean opens the door wider and Jane walks in cautiously. She keeps tucking her sleeve nervously as if she's unsure what she's doing here. The grief is radiating through her eyes. She's not in her right state of mind and Dean is not just going to use it to his advantage, but devour her along with it. He advances to the balcony.

'Would you like something to drink?' he offers, distracting Jane from going further and seeing her own apartment. Dean likes to watch her even if she does something mundane like hanging clothes.

She looks frail and scrawny, with dark circles under her eyes. Dean is the cause of this. On the other end, Dean shines and sparkles. He's clean-shaven and his hair is styled to perfection. I can smell his strong cologne and hair products from where I'm sitting, gazing up at him. He's ready for Hollie and he looks very handsome.

Jane turns and catches Dean studying her but he doesn't break eye contact.

'Coffee would be nice,' she says,

'Sure,' he says. 'Milk and sugar?'

'Milk, no sugar.'

'Sweet enough then.'

She colours slightly and bites her bottom lip. Would the situation be any different if my human wasn't as divine? His looks are what lure women in. He's the devil and they see him as this angel, glorious and miraculous. Jane isn't any different. She fails to see the layers underneath, but I have faith in her. I wonder if she used me as an excuse when she's here for him. Here is this tall, stylish, great looking English man being nice to her while she's all over the place, falling apart by his doing. If she's not careful, Dean will have her eating from the palm of his hand. I watch intently.

'This is a nice apartment,' she says.

'Thanks.'

Jane comes to me and offers me her hand. I detect soap.

'*Hanini*,' she says in Maltese.

I don't know what it means, but it sounds affectionate.

Dean gets to business without wasting his, her, or my time. He's so wise and sly. So skilful. He gives her instructions on how much I eat in a day, my habits, and my toys. She listens and nods. He helps Jane move my things to hers.

'If you'll need anything,' he says, 'or if he gives you a hard time, not that he would, let me know.'

That's exactly what Dean wants her to do.

'I'll pop around in a few days to check up on him,' he continues.

Translation: Dean will come around to learn more about her. To go into her flat and look at her things. How Jane leads her life. He's using me to get to her.

'He must be the most pampered cat,' she laughs.

Dean picks me up and holds me with such care that it makes me doubt he can do so many bad deeds with those hands. I meow as I land in her arms.

'He is,' he says.

The bell goes off and Jane jumps. I feel her heart rate quicken through her shirt. Dean walks over to the door and Jane watches him as if he's a dream. Hollie walks in and Jane looks at her, getting the message that it's time to leave. Hollie raises an eyebrow at Jane and looks up at Dean.

'She's taking Theodore,' he explains.

'Oh,' Hollie says, 'are you getting rid of him?'

'God no!' Dean says. 'She's going to have him for a few days.'

Hollie looks at Jane up and down. 'Whatever,' she says and walks past us.

Hollie places her bag on the counter and removes her jacket, making herself at home.

'I better be going,' Jane says, her face going red in embarrassment.

'Yes, of course,' Dean says, and opens the door for her.

Jane carries me in her arms and before he closes the door, he winks at me.

'Your owner likes women much younger than him, I see, and very pretty too. It seems fitting, of course. He's so gorgeous,' she sighs.

It's obvious she fancies him and Dean has no type that he likes. He only separates women into two categories: the ones he mates with, like Hollie, and the sensible, successful ones he toys with before he kills them.

I take my time exploring her flat. Strangely, none of Matthew's belongings are here. Someone must have cleared them away—his mother, I suppose—before Jane moved back in, so she doesn't have to deal with the trauma all over again. There is a door that's closed. It could have been his office. My favourite places are the chair, where I can stretch my claws on the plush leather, and the sofa. I love to curl on it while she tries to write, but all Jane does is stare at a blank document with the cursor blinking as if it's mocking her. I bring her my ball to play with me to distract her and take her mind off her worries. She places the laptop on the sofa and plays with me dutifully. Her eyes start to water and she holds me in her arms.

'You're like a little angel that came into my life,' she tells me.

She's going to need me for what's to come. I have lots of work to do here. Dean is mischievously trying to manoeuvre his way into her life to destroy it, and I have to stop that from happening.

Dean doesn't come to visit me. I'm curious, however, what he's up to. I'm sure he's spying on us. I'm hoping he will screw up, and Jane will become aware someone has access to everything. He wouldn't make a mistake, though; he's too careful and exact.

Then something happens: Jane disconnects her old phone and blocks it, banishing Dean from having any further access to her social media, emails or manuscripts. Uh-oh. I think he knew deep down she'd do this, and he used me going over to her as a backup plan. Now, he's going to come for her. Jane is going to invite a killer into her home, and she'll be too charmed to notice.

Chapter Thirteen
Dean

Jane has deactivated her old phone; I'm not worried. I'll do this the old-fashioned way. It's easy since Theodore is with her and it's more fun.

Hollie is being obnoxious and I'm losing my patience with her. After Jane had left my apartment with Theodore, she turns to me and says, 'Why was she here?'

Her tone is accusatory as if I owe her an explanation.

'For the cat?' I say plainly.

'Why does she want your cat? Why doesn't she adopt one?' she pouts. 'Or are you going somewhere and she's going to take care of your cat? And why can't I look after him?'

'No offence, but you never acknowledge Theodore and you now suddenly want to take care of him because my neighbour came to collect him?'

'Well, she's not even that pretty,' she snarls.

Hollie is not even fit to shine Jane's shoes. A woman tearing another woman down, how classy. I thought there was a sisterhood going on with women to stick together. The grass is not always so green. Yes, Hollie is pretty with her Brazilian hair treatments and extensions, the fake eyelashes that are so long and so heavy she can barely keep her eyes open. The fake nails and plump lips which she draws on with too much lip liner. I would love to see what she looks like without all of that paint. But this is her armour, I suppose. Hollie is all about Facebook and Instagram. She is so boring. Nothing is interesting about her apart from the sex, at least that is good. But all she is is a show off. Hollie finds me sexy; that's how I was described to her friends. How do I know? I checked her phone when she went to the bathroom as she forgot to take it with her. I have seen her type the password a few times. Her friends complained she's spending too much time with me and becoming obsessed. Maybe I should give Hollie some space and allow her to enjoy her freedom of being young.

'She just lost her husband. Show some respect,' I tell her.

She backs off.

'I don't owe you anything,' I remind her.

Of course, this is my fault. I have should have known this would happen. I was only looking for a shag after killing someone.

'What is that supposed to mean?' she asks.

I open the fridge and take out two bottles of beer before I turn to the cupboard, where the *Succinylcholine* is there waiting. I take out a packet of crisps.

'You should spend time with your friends and have fun,' I point out, closing the cupboard.

'Are you dumping me?'

I open the packet of crisps and pour a few in a bowl. 'What? No!'

Her eyes find the floor. I place the beer and the bowl on the coffee table.

'Come here,' I say.

She obeys like always, so I scoop her up, drop her on the bed and make it up to her. She is so happy, so appreciative of me, of my attention, to be on my bed.

After Hollie left, I lie on the bed, wondering what Jane is doing tucked away in her flat with my cat? My beloved Theodore is in capable hands, for sure. I would kill her before her time is up if something happened to him under her watch. She's like me in many ways: organised and alert. Attentive, but not as precise and exact as I am. I'm a perfectionist, but Jane seems like someone who could be my equal, someone who can complete me in a way. Not that people complete each other, I mean. I am a complete, fully formed man. I don't need a woman to make me feel that way, same goes with women. I turn to my side, considering my options. Maybe I'll give her more time. There are things I don't know about Jane. I don't know what she looks like when she's happy. I don't know what she looks like when she's angry. I don't know what she looks like when she's afraid. What she feels like when being made love to, but I will. I always will. I have been feeling generous lately. I can spare her for the time being.

Jane opens the door and leads the way. She looks better than the last time I saw her. I notice the freckles brushing her nose and her hair is messier than usual. There are boxes by the entrance that make the apartment a little cluttered. On top of the boxes are a pile of photos featuring a slightly younger version of Jane posing. These photos are professionally taken. Was she a model?

A smell of detergent and scented candles mixed with air freshener fills the air. The apartment is small but neat and has a modern and classic touch to it. There is a large dark grey L-shaped sofa where Theodore is lying, peering at me. Behind the sofa is a purple wall. The apartment, apart from the purple wall, has natural colours, classic and elegant. A glass topped coffee table stands in front of the sofa. On top is a candle and a cactus with a pink flower on top that looks like a hat. There are books piled up about writing, another book is facing down, and her laptop is next to it. There is a large bookcase on the other side of the wall that's not organised by book title or author, but by colour. It's photogenic and pretty. I walk up to it and investigate the books with interest. There are books by Stephen King, John Grisham, Agatha Christie, David Baldacci and Daniel Silva. The rest of the names I do not recognise.

I turn away from the shelf. 'You were a model?'

'Yeah, in my twenties,' Jane replies.

'For how long?'

'Not long. It wasn't my thing. I'm not going to bore you with my modelling past. You're here to collect your beloved, aren't you?'

'You're not boring me,' I say. 'And I came to see him. Not collect him.'

Theodore comes to me and I pick him up. Jane folds her hands, then drops them to her side and folds them again, like she doesn't know what to do with herself when

I'm around. She touches her ear; do I make all women this nervous? Or just her?

'Can I get you anything to drink? Tea? Coffee?'

'Coffee.'

She nods and her phone goes off, but she ignores it. I wonder what it's like for her to have a man who isn't her husband being up here. And I am the first man who has been in here since her husband died. Jane is still hurting. For her, it would be like she's betraying Matthew in some way. She's still tied to him. Jane prepares the coffee, asks how I like it, and she brings the mugs over to the kitchen table. Theodore goes under the table and I lift the tablecloth to smile at him. He looks at me with big wide eyes.

Jane tells me what I already know. I tell her what I do, or more precisely, what I pretend to do. She cups the mug with her hands as she listens.

'I always wanted to draw,' she says. 'Unfortunately, I can only make it as far as sticks.'

I guess this is all-uncomfortable for her. Foreign, even. I presume since she had been with her husband for so long and took it for granted the part, where she wouldn't have to go back out there and interact with the members of the opposite sex. To go out on dates, to stand naked in front of another man again. Jane is out of practice and all of this is new and scary to her.

'I'm changing genre,' she says.

'You are? Why?'

'With everything that happened…' she trails off.

'What genre do you plan to write in?'

'Sci-fi.'

'You mean Earth sci-fi or set in space?'

'Earth. Dystopian. That sort of thing.'

'Are you excited?'

'Starting a new genre…' She pauses and taps her fingers against the table. 'Yes, I am in a way. I'm blocked at the moment. It's like I hit a wall, but I'm reading a lot….' She starts pulling a thread from her sweater. 'Sorry, I'm blabbing.'

'You're not. Is Theodore being a good boy?'

'He's a joy.'

Chapter Fourteen
Theodore

I watch how Jane is gazing at Dean in an adoring way. When I was a kitten, Dean took me under his care. He's going to do the same with Jane. He's getting her back on her feet. Meanwhile, Jane and I have become best friends. I sit on her laptop so she can't write and have her attention devoted only on me. I curl on her lap when she's reading. I follow her in every room, and I bring her insects that I catch to show my appreciation, but she tells me not to do that.

'It's not nice, little noodle,' she tells me.

I'll keep doing it either way.

Jane cleans her apartment, if you call what she does cleaning. She moves the furniture, cleans behind it, and obsesses over each fluff on the floor and furniture. I guess this is part of her healing process, removing traces of the past so she can enter into this new life. This apartment has too many memories and they slash through her. Maybe she should move. I think that would do her good, a change of environment. I won't see her again, but it would be okay as long as she's safe. I can live with that. Would Dean still be after her? Knowing how persistent he is, he would. Jane cooks, and the flat smells of delicious aromas while Dean is lurking right across the street watching all of this. Learning, watching, and waiting. Jane moves things around the apartment to make it look different. A vase here and there or moving a chair to a different place. She buys new decor like cushions and carpets and orders lots of books. All part of the healing process. Dean's visits become more frequent.

'It's time to have Theodore back. It's not fair keeping him like this,' Jane tells Dean when he drops by.

'You can have him for as long as you like,' Dean assures her.

She blinks but is unfazed by the strangeness. Doesn't she wonder why? Isn't she a little suspicious? He wants to enter her life. He comes to me and I hiss at him and hide, but he doesn't react to my slight change of mood. He smiles and watches me go under the table. He never asks her how she's feeling, doesn't offer words of comfort or sympathy. Instead, he asks her about her day, avoiding the elephant in the room: Matthew. Jane doesn't talk about him with Dean. Why should she? And why would he ask her about Matthew? He's using himself as a distraction. I have to show her before it's too late.

These meetings inside her flat become outings. I'm not present for those, so I can't say what they talk about or what they do. Dean knows he's dealing with an emotionally fragile woman, but he's patient, that's why he hasn't been caught by the police yet. How can they catch him when all the killings are covered as either as accidents or suicides?

Dean will wait weeks, months, even years if he doesn't get bored. The problem starts when he gets bored. If he does, it means her candle is losing its flame.

It's time for me to go back home. This is all part of the plan. If Jane wants to see me, she can come to us from now on, which she will as she and Dean grow closer. I guess I can call them friends. Jane is still in mourning, because although her face has a rosy glow, she still wears black.

Meanwhile, Dean is slowly getting what he wants. He always gets what he wants. Jane is already involved, and my horror will come to reality. I can't fail again.

Chapter Fifteen
Dean

Jane comes to visit Theodore carrying a small black box in her hand. Sometimes I think that my cat will betray me. I've never seen him bond with anyone apart from me before, and I'm starting to grow a little bit jealous. I am the one who found him and he belongs to me. I gave him a home, nursed him to health and gave him food. Jane only walked into his life just now. She kneels before him, opens the box and produces a red bow tie. Theodore touches it with his paw and starts to play with the strap.

'May I?' she asks me.

'Sure,' I say.

She removes his old blue collar and clips the new one around his neck.

'There. Now you are dressed for the occasion.'

She smiles happily, pleased with herself.

'What occasion would that be?' I ask curiously.

She looks at me. 'Oh, nothing in particular. I thought it was cute.'

'It's very cute,' I agree.

Theodore doesn't agree as he shakes his little head, trying to reach for the collar with his paw.

'Would you like to have dinner sometime?' I ask.

I don't know where it came from and I think I just ruined everything. We'd gone to a coffee shop around the corner twice before. Hardly anything spectacular, but she seemed to relax in my company. I let her do most of the talking. I just listen, never interrupt her, and sometimes, I ask questions to stop an empty silence from falling between us.

There is something about Jane that reminds me of my ex-wife. I met Carol when I was about to graduate from uni. She was a hairdresser. I was too young, and she was already in her thirties. Despite our age differences, we got on. Hiding my true nature from her wasn't hard; I stopped the killings. I met Carol a few weeks after I'd killed Jamie, and I was already on the lookout for another one. I had set my eyes on Vanessa. She was beautiful with long brown hair and long legs. I was in a bar one night and the guy I was drinking with, a fellow student of mine, introduced me to this gorgeous girl, It was Vanessa. We had plenty to drink and we ended up at the back alley of the pub, fucking. It was all straightforward. I lifted her skirt, rammed into her and when it was all over, she thanked me for a wonderful evening and walked off. So the spell was broken and I had to look for someone else. Then I met Carol in a pub where she was with her girlfriends. She wasn't the prettiest flower in the bouquet, but she was charming and had a great sense of humour. I tend to go for intelligence rather than looks. I did pick wrong with Hollie. Things with Carol got serious quickly and I stopped looking for my next killing. I managed, thinking the urge to kill had gone away and it was just a phase in my life. Something terrible I did, but now, it was gone. I hid the notepads of the sketches that I made of the dead girls so Carol wouldn't find them. Although, late at night, after we would make love, I used to go to the study, unlock the drawer of my desk and revisit the drawings.

One night, I went to the study, grabbed my pencil and began to sketch a woman drowned in a bath. I was fooling myself, of course; it wasn't gone, this defect of mine, this monster in my belly. It only went to sleep, and it would be a matter of time before it reawakened.

After three years together, Carol and I got married. A year into the marriage, the monster resurrected, or should I say, someone had aroused it. Her name was Krysten Wilson, the assistant manager of the design company I was working for at the time. I was one of the head designers over there. It was no secret; everybody knew she "fast-tracked" the route to her success. I have nothing against someone who gets help into advancing their career, but Krysten didn't show her worth like everybody else. She wore the power suit without having anything to prove for it. Krysten used to wear those high heels with the red soles from that designer whose name I forgot. I don't know why Krysten used to dress that way when the rest of us wore casual attire. She looked so out of place. Krysten was useless and a disrespectful bitch who thought I worked for her.

'No, you will do these designs now and I want them ready by tomorrow,' she told me once.

'It can't be done by tomorrow.'

'Then tell your useless team to get it done. I don't care if they stay here all night. I want it done.'

That did it for me. 'Why don't tell your useless team to get it done then?' I retorted.

'Hey, I am in charge here,' she said. 'You work for me.'

Like hell I do, I thought. So I took matters in my own hands. I messed up the brakes of her sleek brand new BMW that she paraded around to show us we were all beneath her. No one disrespects me and gets away with it. She and the BMW crashed into a tree. The impact was so powerful, the car exploded. RIP Krysten Wilson. It was nice knowing you.

Carol and I drifted apart, maybe because of the age thing. I met a woman at work called Hannah who was Krysten's replacement; she was younger than me with dark red hair and a loud attitude, but she was fun to be around. I filed for divorce and started a relationship with Hannah. Carol and I tried to remain friendly, though the last phone call wasn't such, and I doubted we'd talk ever again. It was for the best.

Jane's eyes go wide. 'You want to have dinner with me?'

She makes it sound as if I suggested the most ridiculous thing, and I'm embarrassed for my bluntness.

'Yeah, you deserve it,' I say.

'You mean I deserve to be spoiled?' she asks flatly.

Theodore is sitting on the floor watching both of us with a judgemental look.

'Forget it,' I say, standing up.

She stands. 'I mean, I would love to, it's just… you've taken me by surprise that you… never mind.' She pauses and sighs. 'It just feels… too soon.'

Jane never brought her husband up, not even accidentally. She's being careful. Tiptoes around the subject. I wonder if she compares me to him. I don't want to listen to her talk about the man I killed. He wasn't good enough for her. If she stops and thinks about it, she'd realise that. We agree on Friday and I make reservations at a nice fancy restaurant. Not to impress her, but because she truly deserves it.

Meanwhile, Hollie comes over after work. She kicks off her shoes and throws her bag on the sofa, making herself quite at home. She runs her hand through her thick long hair and sighs.

'Had such a bad day today,' she says.

'What happened?'

'Stuff at work. Clients are such assholes sometimes.'

I smile and she crosses her arms under her chest with a huff.

'Why don't you go out with me?' she snaps.

I look at her mockingly. 'Go out with you?'

'Yeah, are you ashamed of me or something?' she snarls.

I laugh and gaze at her darkly. I have been sloppy with this girl. I should have gone for someone older, more mature, who understands what no strings attached means. I don't plan to kill her; I can't kill her. I would be stupid if I do. Neighbours have seen her coming in and out of this apartment as if it is a cheap hotel. She told her friends about me. She might have posted a selfie in this apartment despite me saying not to do that. Jane have seen her. Killing her would be stupid, no matter how accidental I'd make it look.

'No, I'm not ashamed of you, but I thought I was clear from the start that we are not a couple; this is not a romantic relationship where you can parade me around and show me off to your friends.'

She flips her hair and stands. 'Dean, you are hot and all, but you think too highly of yourself.'

I laugh. 'Thanks for the heads up.'

'I just…'

'You just what?' I hiss.

I can't take it out on this girl because I was looking for someone to fool around with. It's not her fault I picked badly. *Take it like a man, damn it. Don't give her any reasons to be spooked.*

'I'm sorry. I'm tired, forgive me,' I say.

She relaxes a little.

'You know I care about you, right?' I lie.

'Yes…'

I open my arms for her. 'Come here.'

Hollie comes to me and I envelop her into a hug.

Chapter Sixteen
Dean

I wait for Jane outside my apartment as she instructed. The air is crisp and breezy, but not cold. I let Jane run the show. Let her decide and be in charge. As if I'm happy to go along with whatever she decides. I check my phone, not that there is anything to check, mainly emails from my clients. There are few texts from Hollie telling me how much she loves me. She sent me a picture of herself lying sensually on the bed wearing nothing but a lacy thong with a caption that says,

I miss you xxxxxx

I sigh and type a quick reply. *I miss you too xxx.*

I don't miss her. She's so boring and ordinary, but it will be over soon. The lobby door opens and I do a double-take as I shove my phone along with the trashy selfie in my pocket. Gracefully, Jane comes down the steps. She did go through a lot of trouble tonight and boy, isn't she a sight. The black is gone. Jane is dressed in a light pink lace dress, and her hair is up with carefully applied makeup. Her heels clack on the ground when she crosses the street towards me. When she asked me for the dress code, I told her formal, but I didn't think she would look like a temple. An empire. A queen. Is Jane the type of woman who sends naked selfies to men? I doubt it. She has class.

'You're beautiful,' I say and give her a peck on the cheek.

She smiles. 'That makes the two of us.' She links her arm through mine. 'So, where are you taking me?'

'You'll see.'

She unlinks her arm and giggles nervously as the taxi comes for us.

'I do drive, you know. I have a car.'

'No,' I say, opening the car door for her. 'Tonight, is all about you. How are you feeling?' I ask her, keeping my voice low.

'It's… hard… since Matthew's passing… I feel like life has become so strange, different.' She looks out the window and sighs. 'But I'll get there. I have to.'

I take her to restaurant called *Lord Nelson,* located in the lovely village in Mosta, where there is a round famous church known as the *Rotunda.* A bomb had pierced and entered the dome during the Second Great War. There was a congregation of three hundred people while this had happened, but the bomb did not explode. It's considered a miracle. Maybe it was. Maybe the bomb didn't explode because it was defective.

As soon as we step out of the car and Jane sees the blue door and the sign with the restaurant name, she turns to me.

'I always wanted to go to this place,' she smiles.

'Lucky me,' I say.

'You shouldn't have. This place is expensive.'

'Don't worry about it.'

We are escorted to the table and sit across from each other. I order a beer and she orders a gin and tonic.

'I haven't done this in a long time,' she says.

'Which one? Dining out or going out with a man?'

'Both,' she replies and blushes.

'How long did you know him?'

Jane glances at the window. 'We had been married for three years, but we had been together for ten years before that.'

I nod. That is a long time. The waiter arrives with our welcome drinks and asks if we like some water.

'Still water,' I say.

'How did you two meet?' I ask. 'You don't have to tell me if it's too… personal.'

'We met through friends in a club.'

'In here?'

'Yes, in Paceville, when it was still cool.' She makes finger quotes around "cool". 'A friend of mine knew his friend and we got talking, then we went outside to smoke.

Well, the smoke was an excuse. It was more to get fresh air. The clubs feels so claustrophobic to me.'

'You don't like clubbing?'

'Not really. I was relieved…' She trails off and runs her hand on the tablecloth.

'Relieved?' I asked.

'When Matthew and I were steady, I was relieved I didn't have to be part of that scene anymore. It's exhausting to dress up in heels that make your feet hate you, the loud music, the chat up lines. Oh God, the chat up lines.'

I lean forward. 'What's the cheesiest chat up line a man has ever said to you?'

'Is your dad a thief? Because he stole the stars and put them into your eyes. Eeek,' she cringes.

I laugh and open the menu and Jane does the same, studying it and wrinkling her nose; I'm not sure if it's about the prices. I adopt a vegetarian dish.

'What are you having? I can't decide,' she says.

I tell her. Both vegetarian starter and main course.

'Dean, are you a vegetarian?'

'I am.'

'Oh. I considered going vegetarian, but I can't seem to do it. You know what? I'll have what you're having. Maybe I'll try this vegetarian thing.'

She chooses the wine and the waiter comes to take our order. After the wine glasses are filled, Jane leans closer.

'Why did you move? I would give anything to live in England,' she says.

'Are you sure?'

'Yes, I love it, the country. London. Ah, London, such an incredible city, the literature, the bands that came out of there. I even love the weather.'

'Are you sure?' I ask her again.

She laughs, which is throaty and genuine. It's infectious.

'I am.'

'And if you would have to pick one place in England to live, where would it be?'

'Cornwall,' she says without missing a beat.

'Cornwall,' I repeat, considering this. 'Expensive, but beautiful.'

'So, tell me, why did you leave?'

'I got fed up, and when Brexit happened, it was a better excuse to leave.'

'Fair enough,' she says.

The evening proceeds with ease. The conversation flows, and so does the wine. I order another bottle. During the dessert, which I pass, but she indulges in, I move the chair next to her.

'So, you have a girlfriend?' she asks.

'Would I be here with you if I did?'

'I don't know... lots of men...' She clears her throat. 'Never mind. So who was that girl that came over?'

I thought she would never ask.

'A girl I was seeing. She's out of the picture now.'

She nods. 'You really have to try this. It is exquisite...'

The night is going remarkably well. Better than I anticipated.

Chapter Seventeen
Theodore

Dean has gone out with Jane tonight. Time passes in a slow stillness as I move to the sofa then go to the bed, then to the chair and back on the sofa. More hours pass and the anxiety grows. I jump off the sofa as voices approach. The front door clicks and the laughter booms in the flat as they walk in. I go cold. This meant that dinner went better than expected. If he brought her here, it means… was she ready to leap into this step in their non-existent relationship? She takes off her shoes. She's making herself comfortable and my body goes tense. She's staying, but she can't! Jane crouches down to pat my head and I rub my body against her. *Leave, get out. Don't make this worse. You're involved, but do not get attached.* Her eyes are glassy and her cheeks are red. Dean pours a glass of white wine and a glass of water. Wine is good for clouding people's judgements, to make them do things they regret in the morning. Dean hands her the glass and she takes a sip. I stand between them as if I can separate them, but Dean takes her hand and leads her to the living room. Someone is playing music in another block of flats. I don't know what it is, but it's an orchestral piece, a happy tune. Even this calming song doesn't sooth my anxiety about what's to come. The dread leaps into my bones.

'Oh, I love this song!' she cries and jumps up on her feet, taking Dean's hand.

'Err… I'm not much of a dancer,' he says

'Don't worry.'

The wine has gone to her head and Jane is about to sink into a bottomless well. I don't know if this last sip makes her like this or the one before that. I climb on the coffee table. They're too focused on each other to pay attention to me. Dean is a master manipulator. A seducer, and he's making her think she's the one in charge, but it's clear who is. I can't stand it, him toying with her like this. Leading her on, making Jane think this is blooming into something that doesn't even exist. She needs a distraction, something to make her wake up from this spell he's casting on her. I walk to her wine glass. She has had enough of this. I knock the glass over with my body. The glass tips over and I watch it in slow motion float in the air, the liquid splashing on the floor and the glass landing after it, smashing into a thousand pieces. The sound makes me hop away and hide under the table. It worked, as they break apart and glance at the broken glass. Dean sighs, knowing it's me. Probably cursing my very existence. *Now's your chance. Go. Get out of here. Go home and sleep it off.* Dean starts to pick up the glass piece by piece, careful not to cut his hand. Those blue eyes cut through me and I see it. It's only for a second, but the glare is so inhuman, empty. There is no soul in those eyes. Jane stands there as if contemplating her life choices, then runs her hands over her stomach as if she's having a tummy ache and crosses the room. Dean goes to her as Jane collects her shoes. I can't make out what they're saying as they're whispering. She turns and opens the door. My body shakes in pleasure. The door closes, and I wait to be scolded. But nothing happens. She is still here. I don't know what happens next, either she stumbles to him or reaches for him, but they're kissing passionately. I had faith in Jane. Women like Jane are smart; they analyse things, overthink and consider their actions. She's not thinking straight. Here is my human, making himself desirable to her, being this perfect gentleman, attentive to her and her needs. A white knight as if she's a damsel in distress in need of rescuing. I offered her a rescue already. I am the white knight, not him! I assume this is how alcohol makes you feel: reckless and unable to reason things out. She removes his blazer, dropping it on the floor, and I can't believe I'm witnessing this disaster. She untucks his black t-shirt from his trousers. In her drunkenness, Jane becomes passionate, exuberant and excited, and she's falling into the abyss. The more she melts into him, the deeper she'll plummet.

They move to the bedroom and he slams the door. That slam was his message that he won and I failed. And I have, miserably, in fact. I sit in front of the bedroom door and meow. Not that it would be of any use. Humans and their privacy. It's not like Dean or Jane are going to stop from consummating their relationship to come and comfort a distressed little me. I can wait when there are more pressing matters at hand. He's the devil. He's evil.

Rays of the sun glare through the window when the bedroom door opens and Jane tiptoes out of the room. Her hair is down now and her makeup is slightly smudged under her eyes. Her face is rather raw. She looks exactly like what a human lady should look like after spending the night with a man, I suppose. I meow to her and she presses her finger to her lips to keep me quiet. I meow again and she comes to me and pats my head. Her eyes are bloodshot and her lips are puffy.

'Be a good boy,' she whispers and turns.

Her dress is unzipped from the back. Jane got dressed in a hurry to get out of here. She should have done this hours before, not now when it's too late. I jump off the sofa and follow her, but Jane shuts the door before I can go with her.

Dean wakes up hours later to find me curled on the bed, judging him. He rubs his eyes as if he's dreaming seeing me there. Jane left the door ajar when she left the bedroom. He looks confused, looking around the room and not seeing Jane lying next to him. He sits up, puts on scraps of clothes, and leaves the bedroom. Did he think Jane would be here greeting him with coffee? Ha! I lick my paw as he returns to the bedroom, looking for something.

'What the fuck you're looking at?' he growls.

A few hours later, Dean leaves the apartment and I go to the balcony. A woman is sweeping her step and stops when Dean comes out, her head moving with him. He crosses the street to Jane's flat, pushes the buzzer and waits. He glances over his shoulder and the woman goes on with sweeping. The lobby door opens and Jane appears. He steps inside and the door closes. The drama of humans, if only they lived an uncomplicated life like us. I wonder what the neighbours think, seeing Dean come in and out of her flat. I bet they're formulating stories about them.

Chapter Eighteen
Dean

Things had been going so well; all of my plans were laid out carefully, and I let Jane take the lead. She's the one who made the first move. I'm as angry as I am confused. I didn't plan for *that* to happen. I thought about it, but I wasn't going to act on it. Jane told me it was getting late and she had to go thank me for a lovely evening. She turned, opened the door and stopped as if a thought came to her. Then she was on me, wrapping her arms around me and kissing me.

I go to Jane's flat, punch the buzzer and wait. I glare at the noisy neighbour who's watching me, my hands clenched into fists. She lowers her head and pretends to be sweeping her bloody step. The door opens and Jane appears in black again. I look at her up and down. I know what this is; the black is an armour, a barrier, a means of protection. Isn't it a bit too late for that, Jane? When she had been in my bed so willingly a few hours before? The hypocrisy. So she's back as the grieving widow, but it won't erase what has happened. I bet she came down herself to avoid having me in her flat to be on the safe side. She starts making all sort of excuses.

'I wasn't thinking straight,' she says. 'I'm not ready to take that step.'

'What?' I ask.

'I didn't think a guy like you would be interested in me and last night, well… I got ahead of myself and… I realised I'm not ready.'

'Wait, are you telling me that I should go for women based on my looks? That's such bullshit. I like you and… proved it.'

'Yes, I know… I need more time.'

'Fine, suit yourself,' I say and walk away from her.

Theodore is displeased with me for some unknown reason. What I could possibly have done wrong to make him behave this way? When I try to pat him, he growls, with his tail low, and leaves the room or hides. Honestly, I do think this cat knows everything. Like he can read me. Knows who I am.

A few days later, he stops with his strange behaviour. I watch him studying a fly, his eyes never leaving its prey. He jumps and his sharp claws go to it with deadly precision. He lands on the floor, elegant and graceful even as he hunts. He moves the dead fly with his paw, making sure it's dead, perhaps? His innocent eyes go up to mine.

'Good boy,' I say to him and hand out a treat as a reward.

We're two beautiful predators, him and I, so alike in so many ways. We take our time to catch our prey. We study it carefully before we go for the kill.

I'll make Hollie's wish come true and meet her in public. Given how things are with Jane, I have to avoid any sort of conflict and drama. Jane can't see her coming in and out of my flat; that won't look good, if Jane cares at all, that is. Maybe she doesn't give a damn. Or Jane understands boundaries and respects people's privacy. Would she ask questions now that we have slept together?

Hollie, however, is intrusive and demanding. I walk behind her and I picture myself pushing her into an oncoming car and see her pop like a tomato. It would be a gruesome sight, but we're in Sliema, and it's too crowded here. Too many witnesses. Too many people will miss Hollie. She'd be the end of me if I act. Hollie glances back and smiles and me while I'm fantasising about killing her. As annoying and tiresome as she is, I can't terminate her sad pathetic life. Maybe a man younger than me, more good looking, would sweep this lamb off her feet, but it's not likely to happen; this girl wants me with all of her might. Hollie wants and wants, takes and takes, and I give and I give. My forehead is moist with sweat with the heat, there people are sunbathing and the sound of the sea crashing against the rocks sounds like music while Hollie makes plans and I agree with her every demand. She wants to be seen in public with me because I'm so hot. She wants to see her peers turn green with envy. The one thing I don't agree on is pictures. There will be absolutely no pictures of me anywhere. She always asks why and my answer remains the same: I don't look good in photos. Hollie doesn't buy into my bullshit. We sit on a bench with my arms stretched out.

'But you're so beautiful,' she whines.

I roll my eyes, which are hidden behind my sunglasses. This girl has no interest in me. She's with me for my looks and for what I can give her. She must be eager for me to take her to my place, but it's not going to happen. Not in my place, at least, but sex doesn't have to happen in enclosed places and Hollie knows it. So, I find some hole where I can get this over and done with and get on with my day. When I arrive home, I check my phone, and there is a text message, to my surprise, from Jane.

Just checking in. I don't want this to be awkward between us. Can I see you?

Finally. It had been nearly three weeks. I hadn't contacted her since she said she needed time, and I gave it to her. I didn't want to be pushy. Though I'd be lying if I say I didn't attempt to text her. I typed down the texts, but ended up deleting them or saving them as drafts. I type in a message.

How about I come to you? Just came back home. xx

A reply comes immediately.

Sure, I've got no plans 😊

.

Chapter Nineteen
Theodore

The relationship between Dean and Jane blooms. Like me, Jane has been nourished and nursed. The colour has grown back on her face and her eyes are bright. She's glowing and writing again, all thanks to Dean. They make all sort of plans together and it's too much for my sensitive ears to bear. *It's not real, he's fooling you,* I want to tell her. *He's doing this because you blocked your phone. If it weren't for that, you would have fallen out of the window or hit by a car or whatever creative way he can come up with to commit the crime.* And he's good, my Dean. He plays an Oscar-winning part of the leading man manipulating this poor oblivious woman who doesn't know she's starring in a leading role. I watch how he furthers this seduction when all the while, he's still seeing Hollie. I don't know what he's doing with that girl.

Jane tells him there is a beach she wants to show him, the word 'secluded' echoes in the walls. It's called Slug's Bay, in the whereabouts of Mellieha located on the northern part of the island. There is a long walk through the rocks to get to it, but according to her, it's worth it. 'It's like your tiny pocket beach,' she tells him. It sounded romantic and that make it altogether more devastating. Making plans to go to the beach with the same man who is planning to kill her. He would kill her if given the chance, pull her underwater and would say she drowned.

What if he kills her there?

Jane drives the car out of the garage, not the same car that belonged to her husband, but a new one. She must have sold the other one. I wait with my heart leaping out of my chest. He can do it. There are many ways he can do it; even a car crash would do. The morning turns to afternoon and the sun is blazing now. When the key turns in the lock, I stand on alert. Her laughter echoes through the flat. Their skin is glowing from where the sun has kissed it. I meow and meow with relief that she's breathing air and not lying in a body bag or in the morgue.

It is a happy time for her and a sad one for me. Dean has given her life again, and her fingers fly off the keyboard. If only it isn't tainted with the truth of how it is going to end. When she sleeps over, which is almost every night, Dean would sometimes sit on the armchair and watch her lay there asleep with me on his lap. As if we're two villains in a movie. There is only one villain here and it's not me. I don't know why in movies the villains always have cats. Dean watches how she lays on the bed, her eyes closed, the rise and fall of her chest, the dark hair pouring out onto the pillow like chocolate.

Before Jane comes over, Dean always makes a full house inspection to make sure he hasn't left anything suspicious lying around. This is necessary. I'm waiting for something, to warn her of the level of danger she's in. I know where he keeps his notes and her mobile. I don't know why he keeps it, to be honest. It's not like she's going to unblock it. Everything is in the bathroom above one of the ceiling tiles. I have seen him a few times, placing the items there before she arrives. I have to make her notice, but first Dean has to be out of the flat, and this is the tricky bit. He never leaves the flat when she's here. He wouldn't trust Jane alone in his flat, he's too clever to make such a silly costly mistake.

Jane has exposed a major weakness that Dean can use to his advantage, her back pain. The pain slows her down, or he can give her an extra dose of painkillers, classing it as a woman who was in so much grief for losing her husband that she overdosed. It's perfect. Dean studies the medicine while she lies on the sofa with pillows on her lower back. He takes out the leaflet and reads it, his eyes devouring the words.

'What are you doing?' Jane asks.

'I'm just looking for side effects,' he says tenderly, patting her leg.

Jane thinks nothing of this. She probably thinks he's looking out for her welfare, something someone who's dutiful and caring would do. This is not the case; he's looking at the dosage. He offers to massage her back and she accepts. How can she suspect him when he's the perfect gentleman?

'Why don't you stay over?' he asks her the next morning when he brings her coffee in bed.

I'm lying on the bed by her feet, grooming myself, and stop as I hear him say this. Jane is still sleepy and doesn't register immediately what he's asking of her.

He stands there looking innocently at her, waiting for a response.

'I'm sorry, what?' she asks after she's hit with a dose of caffeine.

'Why don't you stay over?' he repeats.

'Stay over? Today?' she asks, making no effort to mask her surprise.

'No, for a few days.'

This is too much, too soon. She takes another sip of coffee, taking it all in.

'What about my writing? I have to publish a book in a month.'

'You can bring your laptop here.'

She places the mug on the bedside table. 'I don't know. I don't want to get in your way and I have so much to do. I can't have any distractions.'

'I'll be out of your way, don't worry. It's nice to know I can be a distraction,' he says with a smile.

'Well, you are,' she says, smiling back at him.

'It would be lovely having you here and I can look after you.'

Her face darkens. 'I don't need you looking after me. I'm pretty capable of taking care of myself.'

He breaks eye contact, not pleased with this response. Jane tries to get up from the bed and winces in pain. Dean tries to help her and she lifts her hand to stop him, but he insists she should lay down and rest.

'You're in pain. You're not going anywhere,' he tells her.

'I need to work,' she argues.

'Don't worry. I'll bring you your laptop. Give me your keys.'

'Dean… I… you're lovely, but…'

'You're not well,' he protests.

They argue back and forth. Jane insists she should go home, but he's adamant she should stay here where he can watch out for her. It goes on for a while, this argument. I watch them, wishing she'd win, but she gives in.

'Come on, it will be fun,' he tells her and kisses the top of her head.

'How will it be fun when I'll be isolated in a room?' she asks.

'You won't be writing all morning and night,' he says. 'You have to take a break once in a while.'

She sighs, running her hand through her hair. 'I suppose so.'

Dean leaves the room and returns with her handbag; it's so spacious and big I can fit in it perfectly. Maybe I should try. Jane takes out her phone and places it on the bed, then finds her keys and gives them to him a bit hesitantly.

'I'll be back soon,' he says.

We listen to him move about in the flat before the front door opens and closes. Jane scoffs and swings her legs on the bed and I go to attack her feet. She laughs. I climb on top of her and curl onto her stomach. Jane watches me and I watch her. Maybe I should give her a signal now. I can jump off the bed and meow to her to come to the bathroom and show her. But no, he'd be quick and she's in too much pain to make her escape.

'Dean is so pushy; I can't say no to him. He doesn't take no for an answer,' she says, stroking my ear. 'I like him, I really do, but sometimes I just wonder what he wants from me.' I stare at her. 'Isn't it odd he never mentions his family or friends? He must have friends, right? And this apartment it's very beautiful, but I don't know, it's so… cold. Lifeless in way, like something is missing… like it needs a soul. Does he bring friends here?'

I go on staring at her.

'I wish I could talk to him about Matthew, but… I don't know… he's rather odd, don't you agree? Why are you looking at me as if you want to tell me something, Theodore? If only you can talk to me right now you're the one who lives with him and knows him.'

She has to know. I leap off the bed and go to the bathroom, stop, sit and meow. Jane is scrolling through her phone. The front door opens and her eyes go to the bedroom door. With his footsteps coming towards the bedroom, Jane places the mobile under the pillow quickly. Does she fear he would look through her phone? He would if she gives him the chance. Dean comes in, holding her laptop under his arm. Jane blinks at him, still unsure about the whole thing, I suppose. The thing with Jane is her eyes display every bit of what she's feeling; she doesn't put on a mask. She's too honest, and while this can be a good thing, in this situation, it works against her. Dean can read her like an open book. She keeps on staring at him, maybe hating him for putting her in this position where he has this authority over her. Or hating herself for giving up so easily or having second thoughts. Jane said she would stay; there is no way she's going to go back on her word now. I think deep down she knows, and from what she had told me while he was gone, Jane is beginning to understand this human. This is a good thing. If Jane looks deep enough, she'll know that behind those great looks and tenderness, it's all an act. He's nothing more than a predator, a piranha disguised as a goldfish, and if Jane dares to talk back or undermine him, there will be trouble. Jane opens the laptop, but it slams back shut. The room falls cold. I see it reflecting on her face; she knows she's in trouble, and is screaming it from the inside.

Dean removes his t-shirt and Jane's pupils are dilated.

'I can't… my back,' she cries.

He takes the laptop from her, eliminating the barrier between them.

'I'll be gentle,' he whispers seductively to her.

I leave the room; there isn't much I can do here.

Chapter Twenty
Dean

'Dean, did you take my pain killers?' Jane asks from the bedroom.

Her irritation is noticeable, even though she tries to cover it. I wonder what is making her irritable - the pain or the fact I asked her to stay here. We had been spending so much great time together. It's a shame that it would end at some point or another. It always does. Nothing lasts, after all. She has been showing me picturesque sights on the island, like that glorious beach. She brought sandwiches and a thermos with coffee. Jane suggested we go there in the morning because in the afternoon, it starts to fill with people who would manage to find the secret beach. We swam, and she applied so much sunscreen she looked like a ghost, which made me laugh. We dipped and fooled around and she wrapped her legs around me while in the water and we kissed. I wanted to take it further, but people started showing up. We made plans to go to Gozo for a weekend and take Theodore along, but nothing has come of it as of yet. I have to remind myself we are not a real couple, although I do enjoy her company. She's intelligent, sweet, but a bit stubborn. Nothing that I can't handle. She's lovely, really.

'No,' I say as I jump back to the present. 'You want me to bring them for you?'

'Yes, if you can please, that would be great,' she says and resumes her typing.

I take the packet of painkillers from her bag. 'How many do you take?'

The typing stops. I can hear her thinking from here, *why doesn't he bring me the bloody packet?*

'Two,' she says before returning to her typing.

I go to the medicine cabinet, taking her painkillers with me. Theodore follows me. He's rather anxious, watching my every move and meowing. I ignore his pleas and remind myself to be careful. I can't get cocky. I need her phone. I want to know what my dear darling Jane is up to. The way she looked at me this morning after I brought her laptop, as if I told her I'm about to slaughter each member of her family, didn't sit well with me. Jane is not like the others, but I never got this close to them either. I watched them, learned about their lives, and then made the accident happen. Jane is smart and can read me if I'm not careful. And if that happens, well, the poor lass is in so much pain, there isn't much she can do. Her back pain slows her down, and I'm too fast and stronger. I could kill her with my bare hands, but I don't want us to end like that. She's adorable, and I like having her around. I look for my sleeping pills, another addition I took from my mum's medicine cabinet. I'm sure they are identical to her pain killers. Three of them will knock out a bull, let alone her. I take out two. Little Jane would be asleep for hours. The image of that drawing of the woman drowned in the bath comes to me. Can I drown Jane in her sleep? Can I make it happen? *No, you chicken shit. You'll be a good boy.* I leave the bathroom and Theodore hisses at me. I stop and look down at him. Frankly, his odd behaviour is starting to piss me off. I crouch down before him.

'The fuck are you hissing at, you four-legged beast? If it weren't for me, you wouldn't have this comfortable life. Living in this beautiful apartment or sleeping on that sofa You'd be starving if not dead,' I whisper to him so Jane won't hear me.

Theodore lowers his body and tail and pads away to the bedroom, not understanding a word I just said, but afraid. Or maybe he did understand. I don't know. What do animals really think of us?

I stand back up and pour Jane a glass of water. She's on the bed typing and doesn't pay any attention to me as I place the glass of water on the bedside table and the two pills. I go back to the living room, switch on the TV, and leave the volume low while I wait.

Theodore hurries out of the bedroom with his tail low as a loud thud comes from the bedroom; I mute the TV, rise and go to check on my damsel in distress. Jane is spread out on the bed in a deep slumber, the laptop face down on the floor. I clap my hands several times close to her face to make sure. She is out cold.

'Sleep tight, sweetheart,' I say, taking the mobile from under the pillow.

It unlocks with a fingerprint. I had seen her a few times to know she had changed her tactic. I reach for her index finger and press it on the phone. I pick up the laptop off the floor, check that it's still intact and take it with me. The laptop isn't even password protected. Oh, Jane, an author who doesn't protect her most prized possession. I'm disappointed; this is all too easy, and I love a good challenge. I go to her phone first, to the settings, and switch off the fingerprint. I can switch it back on once I'm done. I'm guessing she'll be asleep for the next eight hours or so. After that is out of the way, I go to her messages. The last text she sent was to Jack two hours ago.

Jack: Hi, hon, how are you? It feels like I haven't spoken to you in ages. Wait, don't tell me you were abducted by that heartthrob you're keeping all to yourself? You are, aren't you? So not fair.

She replied: *Hi, I'm not so good. I'm in so much pain right now, I can barely move. I'm at his place. He insists I stay here so he can fuss over me.*

Jack: I'm sorry about your back, sweet cheeks. Wish you a speedy recovery. Good on him for taking care of you.

Jane: Is it? I know it's sweet and all but, I feel I'm being hijacked! God, I feel like I'm losing myself with this guy. I like him, I really do. He's gorgeous with a capital G. Sometimes I have a hard time believing it's happening.

Jack: What's happening?

Jane: Oh, you know, me being here spending time with him. I let him take care of me like he's doing now. He takes me to nice places, nice restaurants. I'm letting him pick the food and the wine. He holds my hand. I even let him pay! I'm a bad feminist, aren't I?

Jack: No, he's spoiling you. It's okay to let a man pamper you once in a while. There is nothing wrong with that. I say you're one of the luckiest women on the island right now and you're complaining?

Jane: Oh, I don't know... I'm making up for this by showing him nice places on the island that a few people know about, but Dean, he's so pushy and intense. He just doesn't take no for an answer and it's bugging me. I don't like bossy men. You know me, I like to take my own time and pace.

Jack: Tell him you don't like it.

Jane: Tell him? Ha! That's the joke of the century. I have been telling him. He won't LISTEN!

Jack: If he cares, he will understand. If not, then you know what you have to do.

Jane: What? Stop seeing him? That's too extreme.

Jack: Not stop seeing him, but have a word with him.

Jane: He doesn't take no for an answer.

Jack: What do you mean, Jane? I'm worried. Would you like me to come over and talk?

Jane: I can't.

Jack: What do you mean, you can't? Does he have you locked up or something?

Jane: Would I be talking to you if I were?

Jack: Then what is it?

Jane: He asked me to stay over and I have a feeling I'm not going anywhere not until my back is on the mend.

Jack: Jane, you are a grown-ass woman. If you want to leave, say so and if he won't accept it, that is his problem, not yours. Stand up for yourself.

Jane: You're so right.

Jack: Take care. If you need anything, CALL ME ASAP!

Little sparks of anger ignite the blood in my veins. I have the urge to smash the bloody phone on the wall. *Too intense. Bossy. Pushy.* I had been nothing but dutiful to her, massaging her back, and this is what I get? I scroll up to the previous chats. One chat catches my eye, which dates over two weeks ago.

Jack: When are you going to introduce me to this hunk who's doing such wonderful work on you?

Jane: I don't know.

Jack: You are so selfish, Jane, keeping him all to yourself. You have to learn how to share. 😊

Jane: It's too soon. I don't know what I'm doing, to be honest. I question what I got myself into with this guy.

Jack: Why? Even his cat is purrfect by the sounds of it.

Jane: If I start introducing Dean to friends, it's like I'm making it official and it's not. I find it strange; he came to my life exactly after Matthew passed away. I was all over the place at the time and there he was this stunning man offering me solace and support.

Jack: It's not strange; it's called destiny.

Jane: Jack, you're a romantic softie, but I don't believe in this fluffy stuff. Besides, I'm not over Matthew's death and I miss him and I still love him. I feel like I'm betraying him even if he's gone.

Jack: It's normal to feel that way, but you can't stay alone for the rest of your life!

Jane: Why not? Plenty of women don't remarry after losing their spouses.

Jack: ☹️

Jane: What I'm trying to say is I can't move on, not until I find out what the hell happened.

Jack: What do you mean, hon?

Jane: I do not believe Matthew committed suicide.

Jack: Jane! What are you saying?

Jane: I had been with Matthew for a long time. He was my rock. My moon and stars. Yes, there was a history of depression. Suicidal? NEVER! I'll die trying to prove it. Something happened to Matthew, but he didn't take his own life. I feel it in my gut. I'm never wrong with my instincts.

Jack: Are you trying to say someone…?

Jane: Murdered him? YES!

Jack: OMG Jane that is crazy! Who would want to hurt Matthew?

Jane: I don't know. To kill someone, you'd need a motive.

Jack: Did you go to the police about this?

Jane: Oh yes, as if they are going to take me seriously. I have been writing crime for too long to know the police need evidence. I have none. They'll cross me off as the crazed widow who refuses to get over her husband's death.

Jack: Can we meet up?
Jane: Sure, any time.
Jack: I'll check my schedule and get back to you.
Jane: Xxx

Oh Jane, Jane, Jane. You're too smart for your own good. If only Theodore didn't start going over to her place, none of this would have happened. She wouldn't know of my existence. The cat is not to blame here, I am. I was the one who offered her to take him. I didn't plan this as strategically as I should have. I got cocky with a suspicious woman. Her instinct is never wrong, she said, and she's right. I think about how she looked at me this morning with that accusatory look upon her face. Does she question if I have something to do with her husband's death? She said herself I had stepped in after his passing. What is Jane doing talking to her friend about these things? I'm in a pickle here. Everything said on social media is recorded. Jane has left breadcrumbs and I hate it. I have to be extra vigilant. If I see she's getting too curious, I'll have to end her life in the cleanest way possible. I can play the part of the distraught lover. I have her husband's 'suicide' in my favour. Poor Jane couldn't believe her husband killed himself; she's not willing to accept it and ended her own life. It's plausible, even if the police will look at her social media accounts.

I push this away, go to the bedroom, and check on her. Her legs Lethargically Curl and when I clap, he leaps off. She doesn't move. I go back to her phone settings and set up the fingerprint once again using her index finger to secure it. I place the phone under the pillow where it was.

Theodore is sniffing her laptop and rubbing himself against it, marking it as his. I move him away. For a woman who's so suspicious and writes crime, she should know better than to leave her laptop unprotected like this. I click on the sign-in. The word document is open with the project she's working on, a sort of fantasy sci-fi based novel from what I could tell. She should stick to what she knows. I'm sure it's excellent, and I wish I could take my time to read it, but I'm pressed for time here. She has written 30k already. I have an urge to delete the whole manuscript and wipe it out from the system, including the backups from her Dropbox and Google Drive for saying those things about me. She wouldn't think it was me who did it, but I won't do it. For now, I leave the document open. Google Chrome is open and it's on YouTube. So much for a writer who is on a tight deadline. I go to her bookmarks. She has a list of editors, cover designers, typesetters, all the wonderful stuff. I go to her history. Again, Jane never thought of deleting it, but why should she? This laptop is her haven; no one would bother to look into her history except her. *Wrong.* I scroll down, and it's mostly research relating to her book: Baby name sites, Facebook, Google Analytics. She has another email account apart from her Gmail. Jane uses software that saves all her passwords so she wouldn't have to remember them. *Careless.* Never use software that saves passwords. Never. Period. I go to the software and check her passwords - all of them are her mobile number. Stupid. Never use the same password. She's not bright when it comes to these things. The emails are nothing of importance, mainly marketing companies offering their services. An online course she's taking about digital marketing. I go back to the history and keep on scrolling, not sure what I'm looking for. I reach a month ago. I'm about to give up when something makes me lean forward. My own name jumps at me. There it is in a set of rows. There are too many Dean Carters, but Jane didn't give up easily. The search extended to Google, Facebook profiles, Twitter accounts and Linkedin. I blink as the name of a design company I used to work for shines, Deluxe Designs. How did she…? I had a LinkedIn account as this company requested each employee to have one, but I removed it as soon as I quit working there. What is she doing playing Sherlock Holmes? I click on the messages and see she got in touch with the manager, Kevin Baker.

Jane: Hi, by any chance, did you have someone that goes by the name of Dean Carter working for you?

Kevin: Yes, we had. What is this regarding?

Jane: He applied for a job here in Malta and we look up all the applicants after we have interviewed them. He seems promising.

Kevin: Dean was excellent at his job, always on time, never called in sick. He has an eye for detail. He is a perfectionist.

Jane: So, I assume he wasn't fired?

Kevin: No, he quit. He handed his notice, did the hours that were promised and left in peace. I wrote him a good recommendation letter and gave him a good bonus.

Jane: Thank you.

What is Jane doing sticking her nose in affairs that don't concern her? What is she trying to achieve by doing this? I told her what she needed to know, but women are never satisfied with the information you give them. They have to go behind your back and pry.

Next on her history is an old newspaper article about Krysten Wilson. All it said was that she died in a fatal car crash. I shut the laptop. Will Jane connect the dots? Someone died in a company I used to work at. I come here, and her husband, after all this time, has committed suicide. Jane's life is hanging by a thread.

Chapter Twenty-One
Theodore

Jane's days are numbered. I had to stand and watch Dean drug her with sleeping pills so he could take her phone and laptop. She had been out for hours. I had to make sure she was still breathing, fearing he gave her an extra dose so she never wakes up. I sit on the bed, waiting for her to stir. I stayed out of Dean's way all afternoon. He never spoke to me like that nor made threats. I never thought he'd hurt me. Now, I'm not so sure. I'm fast and light. He wouldn't catch me, at least not right away, but if he does, I'll be part of the body count. I don't even want to think about how many people he killed before he found me. After what he found on Jane's laptop, there is no way he's going to let her live.

Jane opens her eyes and lies there for a while, taking in her surroundings before sitting up, disoriented and confused.

'Oh no!' she mutters, kicking the sheet off her body.

Jane stands up a little too fast and groans in agony, grabs her phone from under the pillow and carries the laptop under her arm. She stalks across the room and opens the door. Dean is in the living room watching TV, pretending that everything is normal when he had spent the afternoon trolling through her stuff. He is angry, but he disguises this, and looks at her innocently as if he did nothing, but Jane is agitated and upset about falling asleep. She bounces to the living room and her wavy hair is wild and messy, her face pale and her eyes wide.

'I'm leaving!' she announces. 'Don't make me change my mind!'

Her voice is frantic, manic even, as if she knew what he had been doing while he knocked her out cold with those pills.

'Jane!' Dean exclaims.

There is a loud bang.

'Fuck!' she shouts.

'Jane, calm down.'

She picks up her laptop and groans in pain.

'What the hell happened? What time is it?' she demands.

'It's a little after seven.'

'Seven in the evening? So I've been asleep for what?'

'Eight hours, nearly nine.'

'Nine hours!' she chuffs. 'I have a deadline and you didn't even consider waking me?'

Her tone is patronising as if he's a halfwit, something he hates.

'You're in pain. You need to rest.'

'Which part of "I have a book to publish in a month" isn't getting into that thick head of yours? I'm behind,' she says, trying to keep calm.

'Then extend the fucking deadline!'

Jane blinks at him, a little perturbed.

'Well… thanks for the hospitality and for being such a gracious host, but I need to go.'

Her voice is full of sarcasm.

'Jane, you're dazed-'

'I don't have time to fuck around. I've wasted enough time already,' she interrupts.

'Are you saying I'm a waste of your precious time? Is that what you're saying? You think my time is not precious because you're a writer and you have books to publish? You think you are more important?'

'That is not what I meant, Jesus! Don't be unfair and unreasonable.'

'You're the one who's being unfair and unreasonable,' he retorts.

She blinks. 'That's not what I meant.'

'Then do me the courtesy and explain!'

'I don't have time,' she replies, opening the door.

'Then go. It's not like you're a famous author!'

Jane is already out the door. If she heard him or not, I'm not sure. I see her from the balcony. Jane doesn't go to her flat, but races to the best to her ability, with her hands on her back, straight down to the garage. A few minutes later, her car appears and she speeds away. Jane is smart enough to know Dean would attempt to go to her. She must have gone to a friend's or to her family to have the peace she deserves and get on with the work that Dean would not allow her to do.

It has been three days and no word from Jane. Dean is allowing her space. I stayed out of his way, hid under the bed, table and chairs each corner that I deem as safe. He spent his days on his laptop, working. I don't want to face his wrath, not after what he had said to me. The more time passes, the worse he's going to become, now with me too.

He doesn't open the balcony for me to go and lay under the sun. He always feeds me though, so that's good. Although my litter is dirty and I hate it. I soil the flat because of that and Dean starts to curse as he grabs the paper towels and cleans up my mess, spraying the floor with bleach.

'Fucking cat,' he grumbles as I hide under the bed.

In the end, he cleans my litter, and when I come next to him to inspect his work, he pets me on the head. He sits on the floor, takes me in his arms and strokes my ear.

'You're the only one I can trust. People are so unreliable,' he says. 'Not you, though. You're a good boy.'

He stands and goes to the kitchen and he urges me to follow him. He opens the cupboard and I climb on the counter as I see him open a packet of treats, and we're back to being friends.

Chapter Twenty-Two
Dean

How did Jane manage to make it this far when I was sure I had all of my tracks covered? I have nothing to worry about; none of the murders are linked to me. Jane doesn't know anything about my past, where I lived in London, and I can always lie if she asks. Knowing her, she would type my name and the location after it on Google. Jane is in hiding again. I think if there is something else, I might have missed it. But I don't think there is. There is no room for error. I have to find a way to stop her from going around and finding out things about me. Jane is convinced her husband didn't kill himself. She's looking for something, a clue, a trace to prove her point.

Jane is a pretty woman and I have seen how men look at her when she walks down the street. I tried to find her from her phone tracker app, but she has it turned off. She might be sloppy when it comes to laptop passwords and security, but she is a challenge. Does Jane suspect I would try to track her and turned it off so I wouldn't be able to find her? Her deadline is in three weeks; she doesn't have the time to dig for stuff about me, but it doesn't put me at ease. Everything was going so well; why did she have to do this?

Jane doesn't make any attempts to get in touch with me, either. I left her roaming free for too long and I'm paying the consequences. Jane may be my downfall if I'm not careful. Maybe she knows I switched her pills or I'm being paranoid, which is new to me. I have always been so confident and in control, but now, it's like it's slipping through my fingers. Is my time up? Will this be the final killing and I'll get caught?

People make all sorts of assumptions when it comes to people like me. Some say the killings can cause sexual arousals or perversions, but I'm not a pervert. I don't break into women's homes or steal their underwear or other personal belongings. That kind of thing always put me off. I have never even taken a peek at Jane's panty drawer. Well, I have. I'd be lying if I said I didn't open the drawer and find the collection of cotton, silk, and laces. But I never took anything of hers. I'm more a visual kind of guy, see how they look on her before I rip them off. I guess I'm normal in that way. Some killers take mementoes from their victims as a sort of tribute. The way I kill is not as personal, as to say, stabbing them. Does it make me worse, that I don't keep anything of my victims? I wonder what my name would be if I ever get caught. I am invisible; would I be nicknamed The Creeper? Or The Secret Killer? How about The Silent Killer? It seems more fitting. Would I have a legion of fan girls like other serial killers f he get caught? Would they send me love letters? Would they think I'm innocent or I'm wrongly accused of my crimes? This thought of warms me of having groupies. Women who are attracted to the danger or women who think they can change people like me.

But these women wouldn't know that my victims didn't know what hit them. They'll be breathing air, have an identity, a part of society until they become a thing, insignificant. So many lonely unloved women going about out there, women who are uncared for, who wouldn't be missed.

I went back into my habits after I adopted Theodore. Julia, Melissa, Jen and Kim were the other four. All brunettes, all career-driven, single women. I watched all four of them, but I didn't take their phone or get as close to them as I'm doing with Jane. Thinking about it, I did get overconfident with Jane and I shouldn't have. I found the four women by browsing corporates sites, most of these sites have photos and a little bio on there. I'd look them up on social media to find out how far they lived from me. I try to seek victims who lived nearby. Julia lived in a tiny flat where the occupants had the habit to never close the communal door. I'd find out where these women lived by going to their work and following them home. Julia was an accountant. Every Friday, she joined her colleagues for after-work drinks. This was my opportunity. I studied her movements carefully; sometimes she used to bring a guy or two to her flat. This always put a smile on my face. It was a cold Friday night in November when I did it. She was slightly worse for wear that night and nearly tripped and fell on her face on the pavement. It made me cringe a little. I put the hoodie over my head and followed her inside. Even after you get used to killing, it's still nerve-wracking. What if something goes wrong? What if she sees me? What if she screams? My heart raced, the blood coursing through my veins like wildfire. I was about to have all the power or lose complete control. There was one way to find out. Would I get away with it this time? Would I have the control? There was no lift in the building. She nearly tripped on the stairs and that was my chance. While she was trying to collect herself, I came from behind and yanked her by the shoulder. She didn't scream, but gasped, and I pushed her off the bannister. There was a thud and the crack of her skull as she landed on the floor below. Her body laid in a weird angle the same way Ann's had long ago. Julia had too much to drink, lost her balance and fell. Melissa and Kim went the same way; the only difference was I used the succinylcholine for the first time on Melissa, and I was amazed by the effect. She was about to scream when the substance curled into her body like a blanket and took over. Those deaths were recreations of my first victim. It was like I wanted to revisit that scene over and over. Paying some sort of homage to it. You'll never forget the first kill, as you don't forget your first kiss or first love. Ann was my first love, so to speak, and my first kill. Jen died the same way as that bitch Krysten. I wanted to redo them to see if the outcome would be different, if I'd get away with it this time or if I'd get caught. I never did.

I do another drawing to give myself something to do. This is same as the other one, a woman in a bath, but this time it is not a bottle of pills for company, but a razor.

More days followed without a single word from Jane. I don't like that Jane is talking about me with her friends. It's not that the talking about me part bothers me, but her suspiciousness. I walk past Jack's make-up studio to take a glimpse at it. The shop is a four-glass-walled room and everything can be seen from outside. I see him waving his hands in the air as he speaks to a client. Jane won't be there; she is not that kind of woman of leisure and I like that she applies her makeup to the bare minimum; it shows her real beauty. Jane doesn't need that much anyway. It's all fake and makeup is like putting on a mask.

Despite all my misgivings about Jane, I'm in a bit of a pickle here. I like her and I enjoy her company. She's beautiful and smart. Then she goes and does something like this. The plan to kill her was clear from the start. I even killed her husband, but now that I got this close to her. The last time I felt this way was when I was waiting to kill Jamie. Is Jane my Ann or Jamie? Maybe I can put a stop to this, be with her instead and forget about what I have done. She wouldn't find out any of the murders are linked to me. I can move on and live a normal life like the one I had with Carol for a few years. Except this wouldn't be for a few years, but perennial. Is it possible? Can I do that?

I walk, walk, and end up in Birkirkara, the largest village on the island. I turn and walk back. The wind rasps on the trees and the streets are deserted. I walk past a tatty bar. A man is sitting on a chair and looks at me as I pass. Hollie sends me a text. I had been so consumed with Jane, I forgot all about her.

Hollie: *You don't want to see me again, do you? You haven't texted me in weeks!*

Dean: *I've been busy, sorry.*

I reread the text, and it sounds cold, but I don't care. Hollie's expiry date had been long overdue.

Hollie: *You are such an arsehole! At least have the decency to tell me you don't want to see me anymore. Not make up excuses! I saw you with the woman who came to pick up your stupid cat.*

When did she see me? Does it matter? No, it doesn't. It's better this way and she called Theodore stupid; that alone makes her undeserving of a reply. The silence is enough to get the message that it's over.

I arrive at my street, a car rumbles by and someone drops something, glass by the sound of it, and it breaks. I look up and spot Jane on the balcony; she's kneeling on the floor, picking the glass up and cursing to herself.

'Jane?'

She places her hand over her head as if something had dropped on it before standing and moving to the railing.

'Hi,' she says.

'Hi… are you alright?'

'Oh, yes, I'm fine… just dropped something.'

'How is your back?'

'It's okay. The pain comes and goes.'

'You should see someone about it.'

Jane shrugs. 'How is Theodore?'

'He's good.'

'I published my book.'

'Congratulations, you should celebrate.'

Another shrug. 'This is not the first book; I'm used to it now.'

'How about I come up there instead of talking from down here?' I suggest.

A pause. 'Okay. I'll buzz you in.'

She's dressed in pyjama pants with a chunky sweater.

'I overreacted the other time, didn't I?' she asks when I walk in.

'A bit,' I say.

'I'm sorry, I was under a lot of stress.' She bites her bottom lip and focuses on something on the floor. 'Dean, you're gorgeous. You're perfect… even your cat is. I think

I have rushed things with you and I'm not prepared for that kind of commitment yet.'

'You sound as if you're breaking up with me.' I say.

'There is nothing to break up,' she says. 'Let's just try and take it slow, okay? Can you do that for me?'

'Sure. Come here,' I say.

I open my arms and she walks right into them.

We agreed to meet at my place, and I promised I'd cook for her. I even bought a nice bottle of wine to go with this dinner date. Jane comes exactly at 7:00 pm and Theodore runs to the door to greet her. She has brought a dessert and a bottle of wine.

'Do you need any help?' she asks.

'It's almost done. Just relax.'

She makes herself comfortable and starts tapping on her phone. I open the cupboard where two sleeping pills are waiting. Jane jumps when I pull the cork out of the wine and places her hand across her chest. She laughs and I smile at her. I pour the wine in the glasses. I reach for one pill, crush it between my thumb and index finger and sprinkle it in with her wine. Theodore is looking up at me. He meows and I smile down at him. I go to Jane and hand her the glass. Theodore goes next to her and she gives him a stroke, which he lovingly accepts. Later, during dinner, Jane starts to yawn.

'I feel so sleepy suddenly,' she says.

'You work yourself too hard,' I say, standing up and taking her empty plate. 'Pudding?'

'I would love some.'

We don't have pudding. She yawns again and I move her to the sofa and offer her a cup of coffee. By the time the kettle boils, she's out. I give her a shake, but she doesn't stir. I take her phone away as I scroll through it and Theodore climbs on my lap. There are a few chats with Jack and Edward, but there is nothing else mentioned about her suspicions. What there is, however, is that she can't help comparing our relationship to that with her late husband. Matthew used to do things that I don't. Matthew was very playful, apparently, joked around called her a monkey and told her how annoying she is. I, on the other hand, have a different approach: I'm funny and make her laugh. Matthew always decided where they should go and Jane sometimes wanted to go to places she likes. It's not that he didn't take her, but it was different. I ask her where she wants to go and now that she has this, Jane doesn't know what places to go to, so I'll take the lead where I take her to nice restaurants, cinemas and bars. Her husband, despite his problems, liked to be around people whilst with me it's just her and I.

It's unfair she tried to compare us.

They are two different men. One was Maltese, the other is English. The lifestyle is different.

Jack agreed with her. I don't like being compared to other men, living or dead.

Chapter Twenty-Three
Theodore

As Dean and I are back to being friends, he is back being Jane's lover. But she has to know the truth. I can't fail again. Jane is too involved, too attached to him and this is too complex for my feline brain. Now that Jane has published her book, she's more relaxed. They spend a lot of time together and I get involved in their activities when they stay in, which is a lot. He reads to her, he holds her hand, massages her back. He cooks for her and she shows him her unpublished manuscripts and lets him read them, which of course, he already has, but reads them anyway. I think he pretends to read them. I can't be sure. He gives her feedback. He proofreads them for her as he's excellent at spotting errors.

'I just love you,' she blurts out one day.

Dean stands and put his arms around her, pulls her to him and kisses her on the mouth. He doesn't say he just loves her. Dean doesn't love her; maybe he is fond of her, but love? How can he love her when he's dead set on killing her?

I watch Jane sink further and further into this quicksand, tangled into this web of seduction and lies. He takes her to the bedroom and at this rate, I fear… I fear… I don't even want to think about it.

Although they spend so much time together, Dean doesn't leave her alone in the flat. Never. As if he knows if he leaves, I will try to show her what's hidden in the bathroom. I wonder if she finds it weird that he doesn't leave the apartment when she's around. What he does is give her the sleeping pills. *Give* is not the right word. Jane doesn't consent to them. She's not even aware she's being given sleeping pills. When she's out cold, Dean takes her mobile and starts to scroll through her messages. I'm sitting on his lap when he does this. My eyes focus on his finger moving on the screen and I want to attack it.

Dean frowns, but I'm not sure if he's angry or not.

It's raining out and it's cold, so I find a warm place to curl up. Dean and Jane have set a date to meet at his place as usual for a pizza and a movie. They lock themselves in the bedroom for a while, then they come out and Jane orders the pizza.

'Do you have wine?' She asks when the pizza is delivered.

He checks in the cupboard. 'No, I don't.'

'I can't believe we drank it all. We're such boozers,' she says.

'It's still early. I'll pop by the shop around the corner I won't be long ten minutes tops.'

I stand to attention as I hear this. He's going to leave and trust her alone in his apartment, even with what it contains.

'Are you sure? It's cold out,' Jane says. 'It's okay, leave it. We'll drink water instead.'

'Nah,' he says, kissing the top of her head. 'I'll be back in a jiffy.'

This jiffy is my chance and I can't screw it up. Who knows when Dean will leave her alone again? She kisses him on the lips as if he's going on a long voyage and won't be back for a while. Jane's in love with him, but what she's about to see will change everything and I'm going to be responsible for it. It's for the best. As soon as the door closes, I climb on the sofa and meow. Jane ignores me, busying herself with her phone. I don't have much time. Dean could walk back through the door any minute. *No, this is the only chance you'll have before you end up dead.* I go to her and scratch her jeans and meow desperately. She looks at me wide-eyed and attempts to lift me, but I don't want to be petted or cuddled. I want to show her. I want her to see. She blinks at me as I walk away, meowing and stopping by the door. I hope the store is closed, and Dean has to go further to buy the wine, to buy me more time.

'What is it, you crazy cat?' she asks.

I go on, howling now, and disappear to the bathroom. I climb on top of the toilet.

'What's wrong?' Jane asks when she enters. 'Are you unwell?'

I sit on the toilet and she stares at me.

'Theodore, sweetheart, why are you being so odd?'

I meow and look up at the ceiling. She looks up then at me, pointing her finger upwards. I reach out my paw to her, indicating yes. I hop off the toilet so she can take over. Jane climbs onto the toilet. Her hands inspect the ceiling tiles, and one of them moves. Concern consumes her face while moving the tile aside, her hands going in. Her eyes are about to pop as she finds something. Her face is serious as Jane holds her old mobile phone.

'What the… how did this…'

She takes out his notes and starts to flip through them, her face going paler and paler as she reads, covering her mouth with her hand while a faint cry comes out of her mouth. She flips more pages as if it's one of her books and can't stop as it gets more devastating, more real, the nightmare enveloping into reality. More turning of pages, trying to guess the outcome that somehow this is some prank, but it isn't. Her hands are trembling.

'Oh my god,' she says, placing her hand on her chest. 'No, no, no. It can't be true.'

Jane looks so white it's like she's going to be sick.

'Theodore…'

She places her hand on her forehead and beads of sweat start to form on her forehead and upper lip. She reads the notes again, flips the pages, reads them again as if somehow, they will change and all of this will have been a nightmare. Her lips are trembling with fear as everything beings to sink in, how grave the situation is. The level of danger she's in. Jane in the flat of a killer. She had been coming here with no realisation that he planned to kill her along. All of it, what she shared with him, is based on a lie. All of her suspicions are confirmed.

'What am I going to do?' she asks. She stands with a sudden willpower. 'I have to get of here. Where is my phone?' She starts to check her pockets.

'I have to take photos of these notes and take them to the police.'

A plan is forming in her head.

'Yes, and I'll stay with my parents for the time being and invent some excuse to Dean. Yes, my mother she's sick and she needs me. It seems plausible, right?' she asks me.

'I won't see you again, but ugh, I'm wasting time here. Where is that phone?'

I detect footsteps and the jiggling of keys. Oh no, he's back. Jane has to move before he finds us like this and kills us both. I meow again, and Jane's head snaps to attention, the fear being replaced by alarm as the key turns in the lock.

Chapter Twenty-Four
Theodore

With the turn of the key, the panic surges further into Jane. Her movements are jerky as she climbs back up onto the toilet, places the phone with his notes back to their place and closes the ceiling tile. Her temples are sleek with sweat, and she's shaking badly, her has dissolved.

'Oh God, oh God, oh God.' She whispers.

'Jane?' Dean calls out. 'I'm back!'

She glances at where his voice came from. Her eyes turn glassy. She needs to think of a way out. I exit the bathroom, and she shuts the door.

'I'm in here!' she shouts from behind the closed door.

There is a slight tremor in her voice, and I hope he doesn't notice it. I go to the living room and Dean is walking cautiously, scanning the flat, then stops and looks at the bathroom door, then down at me. He gives me a smug smirk.

He knows, he knows, he knows.

The toilet flushes. Dean turns and goes to the kitchen, opens a cupboard, and produces the *Succinylcholine*. My body goes ice cold. He opens another drawer. All of this is done in practised calm. I see how this has become a habit for him. He doesn't even stop to consider what he's about to do, as if it's a daily task to be done, another thing to tick off the list. Of course, both he and I know he has done this many times before. I have never seen him kill, though. Maybe he finds it unsuitable for me to witness something so inhumane. Tonight, however, is going to be different. He's going to show me how he does it, or at least how he's going to kill Jane and make her death look accidental. She is in his flat. He takes out a tea towel and pours the substance on it, soaking it. A few drops of the liquid drip onto the floor. I go to where the drop is and it has no scent, odourless like water.

The bathroom door opens, and Jane comes out. Her face is white, so transparent her veins are almost visible.

The pizza box lies abandoned on the coffee table along with the two empty wine glasses.

'Are you alright?' he asks.

There is a hint of concern in his voice, but Jane acts casual, even though what I showed her has shaken her to her very core.

'Yes,' she says, nodding gravely.

He leans her against the wall and kisses her the way lovers do. His final goodbye to her. Jane smiles at him after he backs away. Licking her lips, she moves past him.

'I have to go,' she announces.

He attends to the bottle of wine, a red Maltese Cheval Franc. The bottle has a peculiar oval shape. He opens the same drawer from which he had taken out the tea towel. I growl at him, knowing what he's going to do. He glares at me as he takes out the corkscrew. Jane looks at me, her eyes large and her pupils dilated like mine. He turns his attention to her.

'Why?'

'I just got a call from my mum—she's not feeling well,' she says.

Dean's eyes go to her. The silence is chilling as the corkscrew twists into the cork. Her phone is on the sofa where she left it before I directed her to the bathroom. He's working out how she answered her mother's call when she came out of the bathroom with no phone in her hand and it's lying there neglected on the sofa. Her mother never called, she wasn't sick, and there is no way Jane is going to leave. She is trapped in here with a serial killer and only one of them is coming out alive. Either him or her.

'I'm sorry to hear that,' he says, playing along, not believing her.

I continue to growl, fearful now.

'What's wrong with your mum?'

He pulls the cork from the bottle and with the *pop,* I hide under the table.

'She has vertigo,' Jane replies her as eyes pass at me. 'What is wrong with him?'

I bristle my tail and arch my back as I continue to hiss in fear. Dean casts a sideways glance at me.

'Well, I should go,' she says, turning, and starts to the door.

Jane makes another mistake here; her movements aren't relaxed, but rigid. She takes big steps to the door, almost leaping to it. Dean slides the tea towel off the counter and follows her. I growl as she opens the door. She's close enough to make a run for it, but Dean is too fast, too strong. He grabs her by the waist and with a firm hand, he shuts the door and pulls her to him. A cry comes out of her, but he presses his hand against her mouth to prevent her from screaming. He holds her in place and presses the tea towel to her mouth. I can almost hear his inner dialogue.

We both know there is nothing wrong with your mum; you found something, and you're not going anywhere. You're mine now. And you're going to die like the rest of them.

Jane pushes her body back and Dean lands on the wall, but he doesn't loosen his grip on her. He presses the tea towel tighter to her mouth. Jane groans, sweat breaking on her temples. The fear becomes raw and alive in the apartment. Her hands try to reach for something as she kicks and fights. A vase drops on the floor when they hit the dresser and then another object, both making loud thuds as they fall. He drags her back into the kitchen. Jane stomps on his foot several times and hits him with her elbow. She manages to break free from his grip and runs to the door, but her legs betray her and turn to jelly. Jane walks as if sinking in mud. A whimper comes out of her.

'*Argh*,' she says.

The confusion consumes her about what is happening to her body, losing control over it. She falls on the floor, flat on her belly, and pushes her body forward with her hands. She groans as if in agony but keeps on fighting.

Dean places the tea towel on the counter and runs his hand through his hair, pushing his quiff from his face as he leans against the wall. His chest rises and falls, falls and rises as if he ran a marathon while Jane struggles on. Her left hand goes numb. The apartment smells of her desperation now. Jane lifts her good hand, the only part of her body still functioning, but to no avail. She can't reach the knob of the door, but goes on struggling and fighting and it's exhausting to watch, even for me. Her pleading cries turn mute, her hand goes dead, and she floats and floats and floats.

Chapter Twenty-Five
Theodore

Jane lies face down, breathing heavily, but her body is paralysed. She has put up a fight, but Dean has won. He always wins. His temples are moist with sweat. He taps his hands on the counter a few times, making me cower under the chair. My body rattles with fear and unease.

'Oh, Jane,' Dean says, 'things were going so well - why did you have to ruin it? Do you think I don't know what you have been doing? Going behind my back, asking about me, talking about me with your friends.'

He pours himself a glass of wine, takes a sip and raises the glass, inspecting it like an expert.

'Delicious,' he says. 'The Maltese sure know how to make good wine.'

I build enough courage to go to her. My body is still tense and rigid and my ears are on alert. Her eyes are steady, but not moving. I lick her finger and there is no sound of her breath, but she is alive. I hear her heartbeat. Dean walks over and I run away from him to hide back under the table. He crouches down beside her and runs his hand through her hair.

'I knew this was going to happen, but along the way, I developed an affection towards you. I wanted to get close to you, to know you. Yes, Jane, I killed your husband. You were right; his death wasn't a suicide. I followed him down to the garage, and I used this...' He waves the bottle of *Succinylcholine*. 'I dragged him into the car, and well... you know the rest. He was weak, Jane. You're a strong-willed pretty woman. You need someone who completes you. He put so much pressure on you, and you deserved better.' Dean pauses and runs his hand down her back. 'You deserve someone like me. Someone who can take care of you, treating you as you should be treated. Well, it's not going to happen now.'

He turns her over. She's still immobilised.

'It's terrifying to have your body, to own it, but have no control over it,' Dean says as he picks her up. 'All I wanted was to spend time with you, to keep you close, to watch out after you, to be mine and mine alone. That's not going to happen either. I have no other choice.' He stares at her. 'Why can't you just pretend your life started when you were with me? How can I compete with a dead man? You refuse to let him go. This is, of course, Theodore's doing. He directed you to the bathroom, didn't he? But he's only a cat, a helpless, defenceless little bugger.' His eyes go to me. 'You have been a very, very, *very* naughty boy.'

Dean studies her one more time; there is a look of pity on his face. Jane is making sense of what's going on.

'Too bad,' he says. 'Such a shame. What a waste. Our relationship is like a rose: beautiful, yes, but at the end, a rose has thorns. I loved you. *Almost.*'

He takes her to the bathroom, lays her in the bath and fills it with cold water. He's going to drown her. I growl.

'Shut up, you stupid cat!' he shouts. 'You've done enough for one night.'

His voice booms and echoes in the bathroom. He attempts to chase after me, but I'm too quick and light for him. I move my tail from left to right, hearing the splashing of water. I run back into the bathroom where Dean is kneeling by the tub, but I can't see Jane. I have to act. I can't let another life be taken away. It's like a cycle—it goes on and on, always repeating itself.

The women come before me, the ones I couldn't save. Julia, who was terrified of cats and I don't know why. I tried to get close to her, but she went off screaming, calling for help, to take me away. Take me where, exactly? She ended up scaring me in the progress and I had to run away. Her phobia led her to her demise. She died two weeks after I tried to make a connection with her. There was Melissa, who hated cats and always shooed me away. Then there were Jen and Kim. They thought I was cute; they sometimes gave me food. The cheap sort, not the high-quality stuff Dean gives me. I never touched it; it didn't appeal to my taste buds. They simply couldn't understand what I wanted. Unlike Jane, they didn't invite me into their flat and Dean had never got close to his subjects before. What could I do? I tried I really did. They all follow a pattern. Accidents disguised as murders. So many dead people. Angry sparks inflame my body. Fury for this hate. For his love for violence, to hurt innocent women. He will not kill Jane. Not under my watch, he won't. Not while I'm alive. I leap on to him, my claws digging into his skin. He yelps in pain as he releases his grip on her, and more water splashes on the floor. He reaches for me, but I manage to break free from him. He attempts to come after me, but something happens: his feet slip on the wet tile, causing him to lose his balance. I see it in slow motion, his head getting closer and closer to the solid edge of the tub.

Both of them lie there, Jane on the bath, staring ahead, still not moving, and Dean on the floor, lying face down, blood pouring from the side of his head. I ignore him and stand on my hind feet. Jane's feet are moving, only a little. She's not blinking, her lips are parted, and her hair is wet. The effect is wearing off but slowly. I meow and growl as if it might help, as if someone from the flats below or above would hear me and call the police, but nobody pays attention to a cat. Even if it is in distress. Her eyes are moving sideways and blinking rapidly; she is floating on the water, and her toes are moving, trying to grab the string of the plug. Her eyes plead to me in desperation for help. I climb on the bath and glance at the water and meow. My ears go backwards as a groan fills the room of someone in deep agonizing pain coming from behind me.

Dean is regaining consciousness. My heart thumps. Blood is smeared down the side of his face, cascading onto his shoulders. I hiss at him, arching my back and leaping to attack. He screams as my claws dig into his skin once again. Dean grabs me, yanks me free, and throws me across the room. My body slams on the tiles and I race out of the bathroom. More groans, something drops on the floor, then footsteps stomp into the living room. I lie still.

'Where are you, you little shit? You four-legged fucker!' he roars.

I hide in a darkened corner and pee in fear. His shoes come into view as he sees my pee trailing like a snake from where I'm hiding. I don't know what happens next. There is a thud and Dean lands on the floor face down. Jane is holding a Buddha statue, she hit him on the back of the head. She has gained some power, but only slightly. Dropping the ornament on the floor by her feet, she starts to weep, then holds her stomach and vomits all over the floor. The after effect of the *Succinylcholine*, I suppose. Or the disgust of the situation, what she got herself into, or because of the fear. Her breathing is slow and she lifts her hand as if she is still not familiar with her body. She starts to massage her jaw. It might be another side effect of the muscle relaxant.

'How did you—? You saved... my life,' she says. 'It's like... you... knew.'

Jane picks me up and stumbles out of the apartment. Her feet are too wobbly, so running is not possible. Her hands bang on the neighbour's door.

'Help me, please help!' she yelps. 'Oh God, help me!'

A man opens the door his expression is one of utter surprise and confusion. In front of him stands a wet, shaking, distraught woman holding an equally shaking, frightened cat

Chapter Twenty-Six
Theodore

The kindly neighbour has brought Jane a blanket and wrapped it around her. Her body quivers and spasms as if she's caught in the middle of an earthquake.

'Oh God,' Jane mutters. 'Oh, sweet Jesus.'

Two uniformed officers are the first to arrive. The neighbour points them to Dean's flat and one of them leaves to check. The other comes to Jane. She's holding me tight against her, rocking her body back and forth, muttering words to herself while rubbing her jaw. 'It can't be true. It was a nightmare. It had to be. He was so gentle. No. It can't be true.'

The officer crouches before her.

'What happened?' he asks.

'He... tried... to... kill me,' she manages to say. 'He... tried to... kill... me.'

'Who? Who tried to kill you?' the police officer asks gently as if she would break in half if he raised his voice.

'He... tried... to... kill me...' she repeats.

The police officer looks to me, to her, and up at the neighbour.

'Dean... his name is Dean... he's lying on the floor in the other flat. That's what she told me,' the neighbour says.

'And this Dean is your neighbour?' the police officer asks him.

'Yes, right next door. Fine young man, didn't cause trouble, kept to himself. I never thought he had it in him, but you just don't know with people.'

'And she told you he tried to kill her?'

'Gave me one hell of a fright, urging me to lock the door. The cat saved her life, she said.'

The police officer glances back at me with a raised eyebrow. 'The cat did what? I thought cats only care for themselves!'

'That's what she said, the cat saved her. He belonged to Dean...'

Another suspicious glance is thrown my way and the police officer turns to Jane, who is rocking back and forth, holding me tightly to her.

'Can I have your name, please?' the officer asks Jane.

She tells him.

The other officer walks in, calling for his partner, eyes wide. The second officer leaves without uttering a word. Jane tries to stand but topples. The effect of the *Succinylcholine* hasn't completely worn off yet. The neighbour comes to her, but Jane shakes her head. She carries me with her out of the flat. There are droplets of blood on the corridor. Why there is blood? Jane's face turns grey now as she sees the blood dotting the white marble floor. She drags her feet back to the flat and gasps and my eyes go wide too. For a moment, I think my own eyes are betraying me.

There is the blood on the floor, but there is no Dean.

He's not there.

He's gone.

He's still alive!

Jane slaps her hand to her mouth and screams. The police officer rushes to her to take her out of the flat.

'Oh, God… have mercy on my soul,' Jane whimpers. 'He's going to come after me. He's going to kill me,' she cries. 'He's going to kill us both!'

It's all a spectacle after that. Help comes and there are lots of lights. Meanwhile, Jane and I are taken out of the block. A crowd of people has gathered. Jane is ushered into an ambulance. Without a doubt, this will make the headlines. This is a big deal. They might think this is a case of domestic violence; it looks like that from afar when you don't know what has happened, but it isn't. If it comes out that a serial killer is roaming free, chaos is going to spread on the island. But only I know that Dean is a serial killer.

People attend to Jane's wounds, but she's so out of it with fear, they had to give her a sedative to calm her down. Another ambulance from the animal hospital arrives for me. They separate Jane and me. I fight and bite. I hate vets.

I do not need a hospital. I want to rest and be with Jane. Dean is alive, he's out there, and the police have to find him before he comes for her. I have betrayed him, and he'll come after me too.

I have to spend the night at this hospital. There are other cats and dogs with me. I wait, wondering what will happen to me. If Jane will come for me. But she can't come for me if she's in the hospital and I hate not knowing. Will I be adopted by another family? But I want to be with Jane. A woman comes. She's short and plump and squeals at me when she sees me. I'm not in the mood for attention.

'Oh, what a sweet cat to witness such violence. You poor thing,' she coos.

She picks me up and I meow in distress.

'Oh, I know, sweetheart.'

I don't like being touched by these unknown hands and where is she taking me? I struggle to break free from her grasp, but her grip is strong. She takes me to a carrier, and I meow louder at the sight of it.

'It's okay, honey. You'll be with your owner soon.'

My heart stops. Did Dean come for me? No! He's too smart to do that. Is he in the papers yet? Is there a caption under his picture saying "extremely dangerous"? He won't show his face around here. No, I know this human. He won't make any hasty actions. He's hiding somewhere, tending to his wounds. He'll wait until he heals and when he's stronger, that's when he'll come.

They put me in the carrier and whisk me off in a car. It's morning now and I meow and meow, but no one comes to my aid. There are a few stops, the radio is turned on and switched off a few minutes later as the car stops and the doors open and close. My heart is beating fast. A uniformed man carries me inside a white stone building. He walks along the corridor, turns, climb the stairs and walks through another corridor. Phones are ringing in this room. The man opens another door. Jane is sitting on a chair and rises when she sees me. The man places the carrier on the table and opens it for Jane to pick me up and take me into her arms.

'Theodore,' she says, holding me tightly against her, 'my saviour, my guardian angel.' She kisses the top of my head.

Behind the desk, there is a woman in a black suit. She has brown hair tied into a ponytail and doesn't look much older than Jane. She casts a look at me and her lips stretch into a smile. Jane sits back down on the chair, putting me on her lap. She's wearing what looks like pyjamas. How many days have passed since the incident? Next to the woman is another man, about Dean's age with sandy blonde hair and green eyes wearing a navy-blue suit that looks brand new.

The woman taps on her phone and says, 'I'm Inspector Lydia Falzon with the Criminal Investigation Department. Also with me in the room is inspector Cedrick Micallef. The cat, Theodore, is here now.'

She looks at Jane. 'If you can walk us through step by step what happened?'

'I have been repeating the same thing over and over. What's wrong with you people? Why don't you go out there and find him?' Jane asks, unable to hide the incredulity.

'I understand your frustrations, but I need to know exactly what happened. We're recording it this time,' she says. 'It's best to start from the beginning.'

As Jane being to recount from where she met Dean, her hand goes back and forth, stroking my coat, which is soothing and makes me purr. From to time Lydia passes glances at me.

'And this fellow here,' the man says, pointing his pen at me, 'attacked his owner to save your life, is that correct?'

Jane sighs. 'I know it sounds ridiculous, but he did. If it weren't for Theodore, Dean would have killed me. What is going to happen now?'

'Well,' Lydia starts, 'Dean had fled the scene and we're still looking for him. We did not find the *Succinylcholine* in his apartment and you never reported the phone missing.'

'I didn't think it was a big deal. Phones get lost all the time.' She rubs her forehead. 'He killed my husband - he said so himself.'

'I know this has been traumatising for you,' the young man says in a much gentler tone. 'Please, try to understand what you're telling us. You said Dean Carter confessed he killed your husband, but records state your husband had a history of mental illness and he had taken his own life. How could Dean have killed him?'

'Dean used the *Succinylcholine* on Matthew as well. He put him in a car and made it look like he killed himself,' she says her voice breaking.

Lydia casts a sideways glance at the young man, not happy with his question, I suppose.

'Since Dean knows what he's doing, we're in touch with the police in England to see if possible crimes are connected to him,' Lydia says after Jane finishes. 'Meanwhile, the authorities have been notified and we will use the facial identification software provided for us, thanks to you. The search for Dean has been broadcasted all over media and newspapers. Are you sure you don't have any photographs of him?'

Jane shakes her head. 'He's weird with photos. He told me he doesn't look good in pictures.'

There is a brief silence and Jane bursts into tears.

'I have been so gullible. I'm so ashamed. I should have known something was wrong. I should have known something was off about him.'

The young man hands Jane a box of Kleenex. 'You couldn't have known and you have nothing to be ashamed of. I am going to make it my business to catch the man who did this to you.'

'He looks like a freaking model for God's sake and didn't look good in photos, he said? Silly me,' Jane repeats angrily now.

'You are under a lot of stress and what you have been through is very traumatic. If you like, I can call you a therapist. It helps to talk.'

Jane shakes her head. 'No, it's fine… I just want this over as quickly as possible.'

'I suggest you stay with a loved one for the time being.'

'I'll be staying with my parents.'

'I'll have police cars guarding the house to put your mind at ease.'

Would Dean kill officers of the law to get to us? It wouldn't surprise me.

Chapter Twenty-Seven
Dean

My cat, my own fucking cat, betrayed me. That hurt. That hurt a lot. I woke up a few minutes after the hit I got from Jane. I didn't hear her come out of the bath since I had been dead set on catching Theodore, and I blocked everything and got sloppy. That was a costly mistake. Maybe I am losing my mojo. Now, Jane is roaming free, thinking she's a survivor. Jane and Theodore weren't in the flat when I regained consciousness. The room spun around me and my vision was slightly blurry. The pain was like a black cloud had loomed over me and my ears rang like a bell. I got up on my feet and toppled sideways. I leaned against the wall for a few seconds until the room stopped spinning. The black cloud shifted a little and I started to see clearly. I placed my hand on the back of my head and something was swollen there. I reached for a towel and pressed it against my temple to stop the bleeding, but I had to act quickly. I had to get out of there before the police were called. Luckily, my phone and wallet were already in my pocket, but there were two other things I needed. What were they? The black cloud had returned and pain waved then disappeared. I went to the bedroom and opened the closet. I took my sketching pad and the cash I had stashed away. I took the whole box with me. I went back to the kitchen as the pain throbbed. I reached for the *Succinylcholine*, which was still on the kitchen counter, and placed it in the box. I scanned the room through the pain, oh, the pain. I went to the bathroom and dry swallowed two painkillers. I couldn't take anything else with me or the police would know. I left, taking the tea towel with me and a shoebox with money and a half-full bottle of the *Succinylcholine* as my new possessions and set off into the night. It wasn't my finest moment. I thought of where I could go, but my brain was too fuzzy to think.

I couldn't go to a hospital or see a doctor, but I needed a hot shower and a bed. The rest can wait, and I'd figure it out later. I needed a roof over my head. I remove the SIM card and battery from my phone and throw them in separate bins as I thought about where to go. A hotel seemed like an option, but I couldn't walk in bleeding, and I needed a disguise. People like me leave an impression, and this wasn't the time to be memorable. I spotted someone leaving their house, a woman in a nurse's uniform working the night shift. I waited in a darkened corner until she drove off before throwing a rock through the window. With the smashing of the glass, a dog barked, but no alarm was set off. A light came on from the house across the street where the dog was barking.

The man said something to the dog in Maltese, which I couldn't understand, but from his tone, he didn't sound happy. The man went inside and switched off the lights going back to bed.

I didn't switch on the light, so I almost tripped and fell into something. I let my eyes adjust to the darkness until I located the bathroom. I opened the medicine cabinet and popped two more pain killers, washing them down with tap water, even though the water in Malta is a big no-no. I cleaned up the wound on my temple. There were bruises all over my body and scratches where Theodore had attacked me. I took a shower and I let the water cascade over me while blood went down the drain.

I switched on the bedroom light; it was messy compared to the bathroom, with clothes and shoes scattered everywhere. There were traces of a man living there, from what I had seen in the bathroom. I took a t-shirt, a jacket and a pair of jeans. They were slightly big, but they would do. I took a cap and a pair of sunglasses. Was Jane in a hospital? For a moment, I fantasised about going to Mater Dei and disguising myself as a doctor to finish her off, but that would be too reckless. I needed to lay low for a while and work out a strategy. I cleaned the bathroom and took the towels and my old clothes with me. I left through the window and the dog barked again. No light from the house went on this time. I made a mental note of what I could do. I needed a disguise and a new identity. I couldn't go as Dean Carter for the time being. I knew a person who could supply me with that, but I didn't have a laptop. I was homeless. One thing was for sure - I couldn't stay in public places, although I never let Jane snap a picture of us together. So I have that working to my advantage. The people living in the house I had been in will report the break-in, but I covered all the basics. I counted the cash I had in my wallet; there was enough for a taxi and a ferry to Gozo.

I'm renting a flat in Gozo with my new disguise. I have black hair now and I'm sporting a beard, but I am one of the few men that look terrible with facial hair. The beard makes my skin itch. I hate it and I can't wait to get rid of it, but not yet. I don't go out so it's less risky. I follow what is going on with both amusement and displeasure; it hadn't come out yet, the real truth about me, of what I am. The police don't know about the body count. So many deaths. Unsuspecting deaths, however, so it's unlikely they'll be traced back to me. What about Krysten? We worked together; would they be able to make a connection? Under what grounds? Journalists will love it though: a serial killer on the loose, but nobody knows what I am apart from Theodore, but the police aren't going to interview a cat. How could he have known? What sort of a fuckery is this? Could cats observe that much? Are they that smart? But of course, they are. They always sit there watching our every move, judging us. They do pick up things and Theodore knew all along. What I am. What I'm capable of. He's God's gift. He's Theodore. A Saint.

I look at my drawings of the girl corpses; what would have Jane thought if she found those? The vivid imagery, the violence. The girl in the bath with the slashed wrist is the grisliest of them all. I can't draw anymore, however; I have one unfinished job, and I can't stand it. Did Jane think she is entitled to Theodore? Did she think he belonged to her? He's an animal; he belongs to neither of us, but he's mine, damn it. She stole him from me and I want him back. I have to finish Jane off, but I need more time.

Chapter Twenty-Eight
Theodore

Every night, Jane wakes up screaming with horror. It becomes a routine of her waking up shaking with terror, dreaming of Dean coming for her. Or dreaming about what happened. Her screams get so loud that they terrify me and I jump off the bed and hide under it. She spends most of her days sitting at the window, looking out, deep in thought. If it's not by the windowsill, it's on the bed. Tears pour down, despite how horrified she is of Dean.

She washes her body over and over. She scrubs it, rubs it until her skin is red and raw. One time her mother walks into her bedroom to bring her a cup of coffee while Jane is getting dressed and is alarmed at how red her skin looks.

'You can't keep doing that to yourself. Look at your skin - it's looks irritated,' her mum exclaimed.

'I'm disgusted, Mum, with myself. I can't believe I let him touch me. Do you know how hard it is to digest?'

'It's not your fault.'

'It is.'

'But how could you have known?'

'All I saw was a gorgeous man who gave me attention. Who fed on my weakness and used it to his advantage. I need a new body. I don't want this body. It doesn't belong to me anymore,' Jane says

Her poor mother does her best to give her all the comfort Jane deserves. Her father wants to kill Dean with his bare hands for doing this to his daughter.

Jane avoids the news, not wanting to know what the press is saying about her. Doesn't want to listen and be reminded over and over. The image of Dean is shown on the news and in newspapers. The police are pleading with anyone who has information about him to come forward or call a special number. Jane is convinced he has fled the country by now. Maybe to Gozo, the sister island of Malta, only a ferry ride away. And Malta is not far from Sicily. He could have taken the ferry there, too, even though identification is needed, but knowing how resourceful

Dean is, he'd have found a way to get a false one. Dean is not the sort of a man who leaves business unfinished; he's too orderly for that. He will finish what he has started. Maybe he won't act right away, and knowing his patience, he'll wait. He'll wait years if need be. Jane and I will live the rest of our lives looking over our shoulders. Living in fear that one day, one day…

Jane gets invitations for TV appearances to discuss her ordeal in talk shows. This makes her so angry.

'Hypocrites, the whole lot of them, trying to profit from something like this,' she grumbles with her parents. 'How can people be so inconsiderate? Nobody cared about me before. Now, everyone wants a piece of me to use what I've been through as a means of entertainment. To talk about it, to be reminded of it, when all I want to do is forget it and put it behind me.'

She can't do that either, not until Dean is caught. Jane will have no peace until he is found. He has taken over her life and appearing on TV, when all this time she kept hidden, would be sending him a message. They want me to come along for those TV appearances: the cat of a killer who saved the life of his victim.

Of course, the media wants a piece of us. People want to see me, this adorable, miraculous, heroic cat who saved the day by turning against the man who took care of him. As I said, cats share a strong bond with their humans and I broke that trust. I chose Jane over Dean.

Jane throws all these invitations out, and when it came out she is an author, her sales quadrupled.

'Unbelievable.' I watch her in earnest as she paces the room. 'Now I'm the bigwig,' she says and looks at me. 'Why can't we be like you? You animals are so wise.'

Journalists manage to contact her, asking her for an interview, all of them bidding for who would get an exclusive. All they get, however, is silence.

'I just want to be left alone… is it too much to ask?' she tells her mother. 'Maybe I should leave this god-forsaken small stupid land where everyone sniffs other people's business. Oh, I can't do that - the police need me here.'

Lydia comes to visit us alone this time. Jane offered to come down to the station, but Lydia told her to stay put and she's comes to her. Lydia, Jane and I sit in the living room.

'Would you like tea or coffee?' Jane offers to the inspector.

'Coffee, please,' Lydia says.

Jane nods and leaves the room to prepare the coffees. I'm curled up on the chair and Lydia peers at me then stands, coming over and crouching before me.

'Cats are usually fearful of any sound… horns, cars, and strangers, but you're not,' she tells me. 'If only you could talk and tell us what you know, what you have seen. That would be one hell of a story to tell.'

I purr in response; Lydia smiles and strokes my ear. Jane returns with a tray, and the inspector stands and goes back to her place.

'How are you feeling?' Lydia asks.

'Would you believe me if I tell you I don't know? I don't know if I can feel anymore,' Jane replies.

'It's been a shock. You will heal in time.'

'Will I?' Jane asks.

'You will. As I said, I can suggest a few groups who can help. I'll leave the cards just in case,' Lydia says and from her jacket pocket, she produces a handful of business cards. After that is out of the way, she takes the mug of coffee.

'I have been doing a lot of research about Dean, and I have rather unsettling news.'

Blood starts to drain from Jane's face. 'What kind of unsettling news?'

Lydia places the mug down on the coffee table and leans forward. 'From the information I got, he doesn't even have a parking ticket. A stable background, good grades at school, never been bullied or suffered abused of any kind. He studied art at the prestigious Royal College of Arts. I spoke to places he worked in; they all said the same thing.' She pauses.

'What did they say?' Jane asks.

'He's exceptional. Never late, never called in sick. He's an exemplary employee.'

'I did speak to his previous employer when I was doing my research on him. I know I shouldn't have, but he never told me anything about his past or about his family and I was... curious. His employer told me the same thing.'

'I spoke to his parents. They are devastated. They have no idea about their son's... misdemeanours.'

Jane shudders and says nothing to this.

Lydia nodded. 'Were you aware Dean was married?'

Jane stares at her with her mouth open. 'Dean was married?'

'Well, divorced. No children. I have spoken to his ex-wife and she told me the same as you did. A gentleman... affectionate, caring man.'

'Why did they divorce if he's so great?'

'She didn't. He did.'

'Oh.'

'His ex-wife is older than him. She met him when he was twenty-two. When she got older, he met a younger woman and left the wife for her. That relationship didn't work. I have been in touch with the ex-girlfriend. She was surprised that he attempted to kill anyone. She described him as a very intense, passionate lover.'

'What happened to that relationship?' Jane asks.

'He ended it to move here.'

'I see.'

There is a brief silence as both women sip their coffees. 'Did he mention any of his past relationships to you?'

'No, he didn't even tell me he was divorced.'

'I'm trying to profile this guy as much as I can.'

'I know, but he didn't mention any past girlfriends to me.' She stops, realising something. Her eyes go wide and glance at me, then at Jane.

'Did you remember something?' Lydia asks.

'Yes… there was a girl in his apartment when I came to pick up Theodore.'

'Can you describe her for me?'

'She was young, with long black hair, lots of makeup. She was petite and curvy she reminded me of that reality star.'

'Which one?' Lydia asks, taking out a notepad and starting to scribble down.

'Kylie Jenner?'

Lydia looks up from the notepad, then continues to write.

'I don't know if he was having a romantic relationship with her or not,' Jane continues. 'He didn't introduce us or anything like that, and he never mentioned anything to me, but maybe you can ask the neighbours. Someone must have seen her.'

'Thank you.'

Jane nods. 'What is the unsettling part?'

Lydia placed the notepad on her lap. 'While I was doing my search, I came across a series of bizarre accidents. Dean either lived or studied or worked there when these accidents happened.' Lydia pauses and flips pages from her notebook. 'When he was seventeen, two blocks from where he lived, there was an accident. A woman fell down the stairs and broke her neck. At the Royal College of Arts, there was another accident. One student was hit by a bus. The victim attended the same classes as Dean.'

'That can't be a coincidence,' Jane says and again, her eyes go wide.

'Do you recall something else?' Lydia says.

'While I was doing my search,' Jane explains, a little embarrassed, 'when I searched the place he used to work, there was the manager who died in a car crash.'

'I'm trying to see if these so-called accidents are connected to him.'

'He killed these poor women, just like he did with my husband, and made them look like accidents.'

'Now, there is no evidence that ties it to him,' Lydia points out. 'As I said, they *could be* accidents.'

'But they are not. At least, I'm sure of Matthew's death. He had a history of mental illness and battled depression, but I know him; he never attempted to take his own life. Dean comes along and my husband suddenly commits suicide! Dean admitted it himself. Every place he went, people died.'

'Jane, you told me you suspected Dean was drugging you. Sleeping pills were found in his apartment and you said there was a time you had been taking pain killers?'

'Yes.'

'Can you describe when this happened again? Take your time and try not to leave anything out.'

Jane starts to tell Lydia about the day Dean had drugged her.

'He was so insistent I'd stay over,' Jane says. 'He was… pushy to the point it made me uncomfortable.'

'Did you tell him that?'

'I tried, but he was so persuasive.' Jane sighs. 'I don't know… that day, it got really weird…'

'In what way?'

'He knew I was in pain and after I agreed to stay over, he bought me my laptop from my apartment, and as I opened it to start to work, he closed it and he… he…'

'What did he do, Jane? I wouldn't ask if it's not relevant to the case.'

'He took off his shirt and, you know, he wanted… *that.*'

Lydia stares at her intently. 'And did you tell him no?'

'I told him I was in pain, but I didn't say no. I think "I'm in pain" is enough to indicate that I wasn't… interested.'

'And he went on seducing you even knowing you were in pain?'

'Yes, he said he'd be… gentle.'

Lydia writes on the notepad. 'Was he gentle?'

Jane's face reddens.

'I wouldn't ask if it wasn't police business, but I need to know these details. I need to get an idea of what I'm dealing with,' Lydia assures her.

Jane nods. 'Yes, he was attentive.'

'But you did it for him, not for you?'

'I wanted it to be over, so yes, I suppose.'

'You know that can be a form of… rape.'

'What? No!' Jane says and wrinkles her nose, looking at the floor. 'He might be a killer, but a rapist?'

'Rape comes in different forms,' Lydia explains. 'You might think of it as a woman walking in a dark alleyway and she's attacked by a stranger, but that's not always the case. Rapes can be by spouses or boyfriends. Because you're in a relationship with someone it doesn't mean it's okay to force a woman. No means no.'

'He didn't do that to me.'

Lydia draws in a breath and lets it out. 'Then what happened?'

'He left me alone… I went on with my writing, but I asked him to bring me my medicine, which he did. After I took them, I slept for most of the day and I woke up confused and in shock. I had a deadline for a book I was publishing.'

'What did you do after that?'

'I left.'

'He made no attempts to stop you?'

'He told me to calm down. He's so confident and self-assured. You know, self-contained and in control. Poised is the right word. I liked that about him. I found it… attractive. He let me go, but we fought because of that. He didn't even bother to wake me, which I found perplexing, knowing I had a deadline. If he cared he would have woken me up, right?'

'What did he say when you asked him about it?'

'He said I needed rest and I should change the deadline if I was behind.'

Lydia shut the notepad and placed it in her inner jacket pocket.

'This has been helpful. I'll try to look further into those accidents.'

'He's not just a killer, is he? He's a serial killer? I had been… oh, God…'

'We can't say until we are sure. Don't jump to the wrong conclusions, but we're dealing with someone who's not only good-looking, but educated, intelligent, resourceful, and immaculate. These qualities make him extremely dangerous.'

Lydia stands, and so does Jane.

'Are there any updates about him?' Jane asks.

'Nothing so far… his mother was a doctor, now retired. I suspect he might have got the *Succinylcholine* from her. I have a call scheduled with her.'

'That explains it,' Jane says.

'What?'

'Where he got it from. He must have taken it without his mother knowing… anything else?'

'A nurse was working the night shift the night he attacked you… and when her husband came home, he found one of the windows broken. The shower was used and they found missing towels and missing clothes…'

It's all coming out now, what my human is. I wonder if the police managed to find out about the other four women he had killed, the ones I failed to save.

Chapter Twenty-Nine
Theodore

Jane has fallen into silence, but she always shows me affection when I come for cuddles and smiles at me with so much love and admiration. But it's like the words are sucked out of her, as if she has said them all. She doesn't write, eats very little and her parents are worried about her. She washes and washes her body as if she can wash away everything. A way to punish herself. She's disgusted with herself. Hates herself for it. But it was never her fault.

One day, Jane brings my carrier when I'm playing with a cotton ball that I pulled out from under the sink. Unlike Jane, I try to keep up my activities and exercise. Jane picks me up and I complain as she puts me in the carrier. Is she taking me away?

'It's okay, honey. There is something I have to do and I need you with me.'

Jane puts me in the passenger seat. I meow and she assures me everything will be fine. It's the police station she goes to. She takes me out of the car and carries me inside, removes the sunglasses and asks the clerk to speak to Inspector Falzon.

'I have been doing some thinking,' Jane says, slumping down into the chair once she's at Lydia's office.

'What have you been thinking?'

'I can't live in fear anymore. I can't spend my life locked up in a house, unable to get on with my life because of… a bad man.'

'I do understand your point, but this is not just any bad man. We're talking about a killer here who might have killed lots of people. You are a witness and when he's caught, we will need you to testify against him. You're the only one who can do that. Theodore can't be put in a stand to testify against his owner.'

'I am his owner now. Dean abandoned him.'

'Theodore is a link between you and him,' Lydia says.

'What do you mean?'

'Dean can make contact with you. Theodore is his cat.'

'He's not his cat. Theodore made it clear.'

'Theodore is an animal. He'd do whatever suits him at the end. It's his natural instinct.'

'I want you to call off the police officers from guarding the house and following me around.'

'What? Jane, I can't-'

'I have to get on with my life. I need to try to put this behind me. I have been blaming myself for too long.'

'Jane, I'm not telling you to put your life on hold, but you'll need protection. What if he comes for you?'

'I have made up my mind. I'm moving out of my parents. When Dean is caught, we'll take it from there.'

Jane sells her old apartment along with the garage and with the money; she buys a small house in H'Attard. It's just me and her now. She gets back to writing and starts working on her next crime novel. Jane doesn't want to hide because of what has happened. Instead, she uses the experience to write about it. Meanwhile, I adjust slowly to my new environment. The house has a garden that gives me room to play and do my hunting. Jane gets an alarm installed in the house, but is it enough?

Chapter Thirty
Dean

Imgarr Harbour is drifting away, becoming smaller and smaller. The engine of the ferry hums and the sea is so blue. So is the sky. So much blue around me, better than grey weather, I suppose. Enough time has passed; I shaved my beard off and no one is taking a second glance at me. Why should they? I'm just another guy on the ferry on his way to Malta. They would probably think I am a tourist since I don't look Maltese at all. The winds whistles gently as the chatter of people fills the air. The weather is cooling off and most of the tourists have gone home so the ferry, although still crowded, is not packed. I go inside the boat to the coffee shop and buy a cup of coffee. I look at the young girl in the black polo shirt preparing it. I keep on staring at her; maybe she feels the heat of my gaze but even as she places the plastic cup on the counter, she won't even meet my eyes. She could have served a gorilla and wouldn't even have noticed. I'm offended. To be honest, it is not so different from the bustling of London. Everyone is wrapped in their own god damn bubble to notice. I have killed in public and I could have easily been seen, but nope. Nothing. I survey the full coffee shop. A blonde woman is sitting on her own, reading the paper. I walk up to her table.

'Excuse me.'

She looks up and her emerald green eyes peer at me. This is the type of woman who would recognise me from the e-fit that didn't do me any justice. It was insulting. My nose was so long I looked like Pinocchio, my eyes too hooded, but at least they got the cheekbones right. This woman reads the paper and from what I can see, she's reading about the recent political scandal.

'Would it be okay if I sit here? Everywhere else is full.'

'Sure,' she says and resumes her reading.

I sit across from her and place the cup down. As the woman flips a page, her thumb and index finger are smudged with the ink from the paper. Her nails are clipped but no nail varnish. Her hair is shoulder length and it's so glossy, it reminds me of shampoo commercials. She's dressed in a white blouse which is unbuttoned a bit too low. I can make out a piece of white lace of her bra. A black pencil skirt. No high heels, but instead, a pair of sensible flats. By her feet sits her bag and a laptop case.

'Are you on a vacation?'

She's still reading when she asks this.

'No.'

Her eyes meet mine. 'You live in Gozo?'

'Yes,' I say. 'You?'

'Yes…' She holds out her hand. 'Sharon,' she says.

I gaze at her hand; shall I use my real name and see the realization sink in? Can I be this bold? Sharon is the type of woman who introduces herself to strange men. Or since she decided I am attractive, there is no harm in doing so. There are no rings on her fingers, but it doesn't matter. Maybe I can ask her to go outside with me and throw her off the boat and watch her drown, but to do that, I need the *Succinylcholine*. There are a lot of things that can go wrong, like someone seeing me. She's a blonde; it is all wrong. I prefer brunettes. I blurt the first name that pops in my head.

'Kevin,' I say.

'And what do you do, Kevin?'

I tell her I am an illustrator. There is no harm in telling her the truth. She's an acccountant who lives in Gozo and is on her way to meet a client. We talk for a while and the boats hum and roar.

'I hope you don't mind me saying, but you have beautiful hair,' I say

'Oh,' she says, placing her hand flatly on her head. 'Thank you. I'm not a natural blonde.'

I raise my eyebrow at this. 'No?'

'I'm a brunette.'

'Ah,' I say.

What a dangerous piece of information to reveal to someone like me. She stands and excuses herself to go to the ladies' room. I finish my coffee and locate the bathroom. The sliding door of the bathroom is open, and a woman walks out while Sharon is washing her hands. I walk in slide the door closed and lock it. She doesn't stop me when I lift her skirt to her waist, drop her panties to her ankles and take her. She moans and I inhale the fruity scent of her shampoo. When it's over, I throw a ball of tissue straight to the bin. *Bingo.* Sharon eases down her skirt, still facing the mirror. She gasps as I move her lovely hair to the side and nibble her ear.

'Thank you,' I whisper. 'I needed that.'

I could have stayed in Gozo. I was safe there with my disguise. I was content in the quiet and filled my stomach with the cheeselets they produce. Nobody would have found me, or it would have taken a while for the police to figure out where I was hiding. Or someone would have sniffed me out; they are a bit into each other's arses, those Gozitans. I have a score to settle, and the first one is Hollie. I'm still paying the price for my mistake. I have read in the newspapers the police have questioned her. I don't know if she came forward or if she was too shocked and kept quiet out of fear, but the police have found out about her. Jane had seen her and the neighbours had also. Someone must have talked, but that's not what I have an issue with. The police were doing their job and she did her duty as a good law-abiding citizen, but what came next was what sent my anger into a new height. Hollie did a lengthy interview for a local magazine, appeared as a guest on a local TV show, spoke to papers and social media. Playing the victim, milking it. Hollie is all about attention, and attention seekers like her have no shame. To shine under the spotlight, to experience a bit of fame. The newspapers, articles and interviews, I read them since they were in English. The TV show she appeared on was in Maltese, but no subtitles were required; the tears and the drama were enough to indicate what she was talking about. I never did anything to that girl; you wouldn't bat your eyelids to a man and say it was abuse. That's not how it works. No Hollie, no. This was her little vendetta for dumping her the way I did. Yes, I did it by text and I was a coward and cruel, but she'll get over it. She didn't and now she was spreading lies about me and this was her great opportunity. What about Jane? She must have gotten hundreds upon hundreds of invitations, and I didn't see her making a spectacle of herself and she is the true victim here, but Jane has grace. Jane has class and she is mature. I would have killed her if she weren't so lucky. Not lucky, but if it weren't for Theodore. She would have been dead.

Did Hollie show them all the slutty selfies she sent me? Of course not. Those selfies are still in my possession. That is the thing with the new age of technology; nothing goes away, no matter how much you click and tap on that delete button. Maybe I can leak those naked selfies anonymously. It's not that hard, but I am a man, not a child, and I won't sink that low. She was never a target, but she made a mistake, a big one. Now she placed herself as an elected one, and I am coming for her.

I get dressed for Hollie. She might be worthless, but I'll give her a good kill to end her sad, pathetic existence. People like her don't live, they exist. I put on a black suit along with a black t-shirt underneath and do my hair. I want to look my absolute best for her, even knowing the outcome is going to get messy. Hollie, it is time for you to shine. She still lives in the same old block of flats in the whereabouts of Msida. Hollie lives with her mother, who is separated from Hollie's father. Her mother is the night manager in the Westin Dragonara, a squawky hotel in St Julian's, and tonight, mummy dearest is at work. Hollie had told me her mother always takes Wednesday and Fridays off. Today is Thursday. I stand outside her street, looking up at her window to make sure she is alone. The lights are on and I make out her shadow from time to time moving about in the room. I wait hoping for another shadow to appear just in case there was a slight change of plan with mummy or she might have a man in there but nope, she is alone. I soak a handkerchief with *Succinylcholine*. A man comes out and I keep my head low as I walk inside. Did she think about the consequences that would follow before exposing her drama to strangers? I knock on the door, and as soon as the door opens, her mouth gapes open, ready to scream, but I leap to her, covering her mouth with my hands and shut the door. I wasn't with Hollie for her high IQ, but she should have considered moving. After all, she told a serial killer where she lived. How stupid can one be to answer the door when that person didn't ring the buzzer? Tears smear down her cheeks, her hair is wet and face free from makeup. She's dressed in a fluffy white robe. Hollie doesn't need all of that makeup; she is pretty without it. Her eyebrows are still painted, her lips are still plump and she still has eyelash extensions on. With my hand still covering her mouth, I ram her face against the wall and twist both of her hands behind her back.

'Hello, Hollie,' I say. 'Did you think I wouldn't come for you after what you had done?'

'Mmmmm….mmmmm.'

I feed on her fear as I take out the soaked handkerchief and press it firmly to her mouth. She makes a few failed attempts to break free, but she is not a fighter like Jane.

Within minutes, Hollie has lost all control of her body. My heart is alive and an electric sensation fills my body that is almost euphoric. I start to fill the bath with warm water. I go to her and she's lying limply on the floor, unable to move, but her eyes are open and making sense of what is going on.

I crouch down beside her. 'Why couldn't you just keep your mouth shut? None of this would have happened. You were never a target; you were never in danger. Yes, I did think of killing you, but you weren't the right one. Too much drama surrounds you, too many friends, but do you think they will miss you now?'

I pick her up, carry her to the bathroom and lay her in the bath. From my pocket, I produce a razor and place it on the white marble of the tub. She doesn't move and I feel like God to have this power, this much control.

'You know what I never liked about you, Hollie? It's not the selfies and all of that nonsense, but the fact you never liked Theodore. He is part of me, do you understand that? I heard you call him stupid more than once and I didn't like that very much.'

She can't answer me, but I can hear her in her mind telling me, *but even your own cat wants nothing to do with you. He has chosen someone else over you. What do you have to say about that, you son of a bitch?*

I smile. God knows what she's thinking about. She's terrified, and fear does make the brain unable to think straight, but that's what I can hear her say.

'How does it feel, now that it's me, the last person you'll ever see, your ever so beautiful Dean? I wish I could hear you beg and plead for your life, but you wouldn't get that chance now. You made your choice. Remember this, little bird: I am not the one who is going to kill you, but you killed yourself from the moment you stepped out and started to talk about our relationship.'

I pick up the razor and reach for her hand. The blue veins are spidering up her wrist and with one quick swift move, I swipe it through her skin. There is a little bit of red at first swimming like an eel in the bath. I wrinkle my nose at the sight; the red is painting her robe. I stop to see if I feel something. Maybe the little boy in me would come forward and grimace at this sight. But nothing comes. Only that disease in me feeding. Her mum is going to find a nice surprise when she gets home. The police will know this is my handy work, no doubt about that, and to be honest, I am not bothered. Let them come.

I grab her other hand and sink in the razor to her flesh. The water goes maroon, almost brown. I close the tap. Hollie is already unconscious, and in less than ten minutes, she'll be dead.

Chapter Thirty-One
Theodore

Jane sleeps with a knife under her pillow. At night, it's when I get the most vulnerable, and I don't sleep a wink. We both jump with each sound. We still live-in fear and sometimes, I sense him. Like he's nearby watching us. I don't detect his smell, however. Jane goes on glancing over her shoulder, our minds not yet put at ease. Will they ever be? Her parents were against the idea of her living alone in a house without any protection. It's like she's waiting for him to come to us. Her way of calling for him.

Jane is back from her shopping and I go by the door to greet her. I follow her with my tail upwards. Jane starts to put away the purchases while I watch her, sitting on the top of the counter. When this chore is done, Jane turns, smiles and pats my head.

'So cute. It's illegal to be this cute,' she tells me.

She turns on the gas and there is a puff of the orange-blue flame as she puts the kettle on. From another bag, she takes out a dress. It has a light colour with florals. She takes the dress with her and goes upstairs. I listen to the squawking sound of the bedroom door and the hangers moving. I climb on the window and watch the house sparrows fly about, wishing I could catch one. There is a small sound coming from the kitchen. My ears move. It's a sound so faint, it's not detectable to humans, but I can hear it. I turn my head towards the kitchen, but it's empty. Something is odd, though: the laptop has come to life. The screen was dark before Jane went upstairs. I meow, sensing something is not right, but not sure what exactly.

'It's okay, honey, I'm here,' Jane says from the bedroom now.

But the smell becomes real. A pair of fingers start to stroke my head and from the reflection of the window, I see him.

He's back.
He's back.
He's back.

'Hello, Theodore,' Dean whispers. 'Did you think I'd forget about you after what you had done?'

He moves a chair and sits down. I climb on the other chair opposite of him. 'You always had been an amusing little fellow,' he hushes. 'I see you settled comfortably here. You hurt me, little guy. What you did hurt a lot,' Dean continues in a low voice. 'I saved you and you chose her,' he indicates with his head to the upstairs, 'over me.'

I stare at him as if I have no idea what he's saying.

'You can understand me, can't you? You are not like most cats. You are not ordinary. You're a Theodore. Oh yes, you do, you can understand me quite clearly.'

The kettle starts to whistle. He looks at the kitchen and footsteps are moving above us. Dean gestures for me to be quiet stands and walks in the kitchen. He's back to finish the job. Why didn't the alarm go off? Did Dean figure out the code somehow? He fiddles with her laptop.

'Old habits die hard,' he mutters under his breath.

Jane has changed from her jeans and jumper to a white dress and green cardigan. She comes down the stairs with her hand placed on her lower back. Jane has been having back pain again lately and if she's in pain right now, it is not going to help her not with what's to come. I howl at the sight of her to warn her.

'Yes, Theodore, I'll give you your treat soon,' she says, making it to the kitchen.

She turns off the gas and takes out the mug from the cupboard. I run to the kitchen, yowling. It seems to register now that I don't do this. I never had done this since that night he nearly killed her.

She looks down at me. 'What's wrong, Theodore?'

Her eyes are wide and glassy. I climb on the granite counter of the kitchen near her laptop. Jane's face goes pale and the horror appears from her face. Dean has changed her desktop wallpaper to a painting of a man sitting on the chair and a woman lying down on the floor. Dead by the look of it. Seeing this, Jane places her hand to her mouth. To me it looks like any other picture, although

I admit it looks it looks dark and disturbing. But to Jane, it means something else entirely.

'Ezzelin and Meduna …' she whispers.

Jane sees Dean in the steel of the kettle, standing behind her. She screams, knocking the kettle over with the bang as I scatter away under the table. Dean's face remains impassive.

'Hello, Jane.'

Jane places her hand on the counter as if to balance herself, too terrified to utter a word, to see him standing there looking like his former handsome self, dressed in a black suit. He comes to her and she recoils away.

'I'm not going to hurt you,' he says gently.

Tears water her eyes. He leads her to the table and placing both his hands on her shoulders, pulls her down to sit.

'You have been well, I see,' he says.

Jane starts to cry, but nods to give him a response.

'Would you like some tea?'

She nods.

Dean picks up the kettle off the floor. Although most of the water has spilled, he places the kettle back on. I watch him closely. He opens the cupboard where the mugs are. How does he know?

'This is what I find odd,' Dean says, opening the drawer where the cutlery is.

How does he know where everything is? It's like he had been living here with us. Jane watches me closely, probably wondering the same thing.

'Why living alone? Did you think I wouldn't come for you?'

Jane wipes her eyes with her fingers, trying to get past the horror. Her body is trembling now.

'I'm not afraid of you,' she says in a low tone.

He chuckles. 'No? You look pretty terrified right now.'

He places the tea in front of her and sits in the chair next to her. Jane looks at the steaming mug, and Dean takes it from in front of her, knowing what she wanted to do with it.

'Relax, Jane. This is a friendly visit.'

'How did you get in?'

He taps his finger against the table. 'That was easy.'

Jane starts to fumble for something under the table.

'Was it?'

'Yes. You know how resourceful I can be… did you think an alarm was going to keep you safe?'

She averts her eyes. 'You killed so many people… you would have killed me.'

'Now, Jane, let's not get too dramatic. You were going to leave after what Theodore directed you to. I still can't get over how he managed to do that, but he has always been a clever boy.'

'Of course I was going to leave. You planned to kill me all along.'

He waves a finger at her. 'That's where you're wrong, my love. I admit, yes, I wanted to kill you at first. I elected you just like the others.'

'The others?' she asks.

'Oh, you didn't know? The police over here didn't figure that out?' he says smugly now. 'I have killed four women back in England, but I covered my tracks too well to link them to me. I'm not here to brag about my killings. I came to see you. Along the way, I grew fond of you, so I decided to spare you only and only if you wouldn't leave. Your mistake was you tried to leave, so…'

'Did you expect me to stay with you knowing you were planning on killing me? Everything, all of it, was a lie. Do you have any idea… what did you do to me? I would have been better off if you killed me.'

'Yes, and I'm so sorry.'

She looks at him as if he's mad.

'Sorry? You killed Matthew! You killed my husband!' Jane says, standing.

Dean jumps up, reaches for her and pulls her against the wall, his face inches from hers.

'Matthew, Matthew, Matthew. Let him go already. He wasn't good for you. He treated you as if you were his nurse and cleaning lady. You deserve much better than that!'

'Really? You? You disgust me.'

He pushes her harder against the wall and a strange sound comes out of her like a hiccup.

'Do I now? I didn't hear you telling me that when we were in bed together. I'll always be a part of you. And no matter how much it revolts you, I was inside you.'

She slides down the wall in a crouched position, covering her face with her hands, weeping. Jane is shaking so hard I think she's about to break. I hiss at him.

'Oh, shut up, you four-legged beast,' he says to me.

He grabs Jane by the waist, who's sobbing now. He makes her stand.

'I'm sorry,' he whispers. 'I didn't mean to be vulgar.'

He wipes her tears with his thumb and kisses her. I can't stand it. I climb on the table. He places one hand on Jane's neck and points his finger at me with the other one.

'No more surprises,' he says to me. 'You try to attempt what you did again and I will snap your little neck.'

His threats won't work on me.

'No!' Jane cries.

He looks at her. 'I'm not going to kill him. I'm not that kind of monster. I don't hurt animals, children or old people. I just kill a few times. It's a vice: you smoke and I kill. It's the same. Smoking kills too, Jane. You know that.'

Jane's eyes are so wide they look like saucers.

'Why did you pick this house?' he continues. 'Since you're running from me, you should have picked a more crowded place, not a secluded house in a quiet village. You called off the police protection. You like to go in hiding, but I thought you would be much smarter this time. But you left a trail of breadcrumbs, Jane. You have a useless alarm system and I spotted the bat by the front door and the knife under the pillow. You must have been scared, living here on your own. It's not a wise decision.'

Jane's chest rises and falls and she doesn't give him a reply.

The room turns icy.

'What did you buy today?' he asks casually.

The rise and fall of her chest stops. 'What?'

'Did you buy a new dress, Jane?'

Another strange noise comes out of her mouth and Dean laughs.

'Let's see what you bought, shall we?' he says and leads Jane out of the kitchen, down to the hallway and up the stairs.

I trail behind them as Dean pushes Jane down on the bed and she looks around the room frantically. Dean flips the closet door open and emerges with her clothes. He turns and Jane glances at him.

'Do you still have the dress you wore when I took you out?'

'We have been out a lot of times. I don't know which dress you're referring to.'

'Oh, come on now, you are breaking my heart.'

'You have no heart,' she says.

He glares at her and Jane realises her mistake. Provoking him is a bad idea. Jane breaks eye contact and clears her throat.

'You mean the pink dress when we went out for dinner for the first time?'

'Now, that's better,' he says. 'Yes, that's the one. You looked stunning. You dressed up for me, didn't you? I took you to a place you always wanted to go. I bet your precious Matthew didn't take you there now, did he?'

She doesn't give him a response.

'Did he?' he asks, raising his voice.

She jumps. 'No.'

'Just as I thought. So where is the dress?'

'Sorry, I threw it away,' she says.

'Shame,' Dean says as he pulls out the new dress she had bought and throws it at her. 'Put it on.'

It wasn't a request, but an order. Jane gazes at the dress while her fingers inspect the hem.

She removes her cardigan as Dean watches her. 'Can't you turn?'

'Why?' he points out.

There's a slight hesitation, then she removes her dress and drops it on the floor. Dean gazes at her. I lay on my stomach on the bed, wondering where this is leading. Does he want her to dress up for him to toy with her? Does he want her to look a particular way before he kills her because that is why he is here? He goes to her, wrapping his hands around her waist and pulling her to him. Jane pulls away from him a little, but he keeps her firmly in place.

'What do you want?' she asks, her voice cracking.

'You. I want you. You're *mine*.'

'Let me go! I won't let you do this to me again.'

I hop off as Dean pushes her on the bed, pinning her down with his knees. Jane cries out.

'What the hell do you mean by again?' he roars.

'Please, you're hurting me.'

'ANSWER ME!'

'That… day… when I had my back pain… you forced me… to have… sex with you knowing…. I was in an inconsiderable amount of pain…. You drugged me afterwards! You switched… my painkillers… with….' she sniffed, 'sleeping pills.'

He removes his knees from her shoulders. Jane rubs them with both hands and attempts to get up from the bed, but with his palm of his hand, he pushes her back down.

'Are you trying to tell me that I am a rapist, Jane?'

'You violated me. That is rape,' she says.

'That's what the detective you have been getting friendly with told you?'

She stares at him then looks at me, her eyes pleading.

'Look at me, Jane.'

She obeys.

'Yes.'

Making him angry is not going to benefit her.

'I was giving you sleeping pills because you were snooping around in things that did not concern you.'

'Why you didn't tell me you were married before?' she says.

He pins her down on the bed. I attack his feet and he tries to kick me, but I leap off the bed.

'Why? Does it matter if I was married or not?'

'You're insane.'

'No, Jane, to commit the crimes that I have and get away with it, you have to be quite sane.'

There is a struggle as she tries to break free. They roll on the bed. I attack his leg with my paws, but he doesn't seem to feel me. They fall off the bed and Jane kicks him. I leap on his back with my claws ready. Dean whines in pain as Jane crawls out of the room. He tries to reach for me, but I jump off him, scattering from the room. Jane sprints to the front door, but it's locked. The panic grabs her.

'Where are the keys?'

Jane always leaves the keys in the bowl by the entrance. They are not there because Dean had taken them. We hear movement coming from upstairs. Jane runs to the kitchen, opens the drawer and pulls it out so fast, the drawer drops on the floor. The bang echoes in the room and I run away. Dean walks in the kitchen and I see him jiggling a pair of keys with his thumb and index finger. The blade of the knife casts a reflection on the kitchen as Jane points it at him.

'Looking for these?' he asks.

'Don't!' she shouts. 'Do not make another move.'

'You want to go down the dramatic route? You know I can overpower you and kill you.'

'Fuck you! How do you plan to do it? Drown me in the bath cover it as a suicide as the heartbroken widow like you did the last time? Now that won't work. Which one is it? Blow up the house with me and Theodore in it?'

'Oh, I have already achieved that.'

'What?'

'Remember Hollie? The little piece I had on the side, well… she's dead now in the bath with her wrists slashed. Yes, it was messy as you can imagine.'

'No…' Jane says. 'Why?'

'Because she was an attention seeker who was telling lies about me.'

My ears perk up and I climb on the windowsill. What took them so long? They need to hurry; the knife slides onto the floor and Dean has Jane again, his hands on her neck, choking her. Again, I leap to him and Jane jerks away. The front door is kicked open and it bangs against the wall. With the gunshot, I sprint past the feet of the police, out of the house and I run as fast as I can go.

Chapter Thirty-Two
Theodore

I go back to the house and Jane is outside, shaken but unharmed. I walk inside the house past the feet and I make him out on the floor with officers surrounding him. I go close to him and lay on his chest. I don't hear a heartbeat; I don't feel the blood splashing in his veins nor his warmth. Dean is stone cold. Curious eyes are upon me as I remain there, curled on his chest. I want to tell him how sorry I am, that I meant for none of this to happen. If he only understood. If only he had stopped. I'm lifted up, which makes me struggle and try to bite into those hands, but I'm ignored and placed into Jane's arms. She holds me close to her. I meow.

'I know, sweetheart, I know. I know you loved him,' she says.

I wasn't fully honest. I guess you can say I lied.

Let's rewind to when Jane went to see Lydia in her office and had taken me along. While Jane was at her parents', it gave her plenty of time to think, looking for ways to lure Dean into a trap. When she told Lydia her plan, the good inspector refused and told her this is not a crime novel; the stakes were too high. And the big guys upstairs would never agree since Jane, apart from being a victim, was a key witness.

'Do you want to catch him?' Jane asked her.

'Yes, but this is dangerous and it won't be authorised.'

'It has been months already and nothing.'

'It takes time.'

'And what you propose I do in the meantime? Put my life on hold? I can't live in fear. I won't allow having my life ruled by a bad man.'

'This isn't just any bad man. He tried to kill you and there is a possibility he's a serial killer.'

'He's brilliant and evil. He's patient, but relentless. This can be his downfall. He won't let a job go unfinished and he has unfinished business with me. I'm not dead yet, so he'll come back to finish me off. Just hear me out, okay? Can you allow me that at least?'

Lydia obliged and Jane began to explain her careful elaborate plan. Lydia applauded Jane for her imagination, but it couldn't be done. It needed a team of officers dressed as civilians watching over the house. Making sure neither Jane nor I would get hurt or worse killed. It was too risky, plain and simple.

Why he came back, knowing he'd be lured into a trap, is something both Jane and I can't fathom. Maybe he got too cocky, so much so that he came during the day, not at night. Alarms systems were set up in the house. There were emergency buttons in the kitchen under the table, the other under one of the cupboards by the cooker that was why Jane leaned her hands on it. These failed as Dean had deactivated all the alarms in the house and the electricity along with it. That was why it took so long for the police to come to our aid because we had no way of signalling them. Dean was shot by Lydia.

So this is my little tale. I have nothing more to add. Jane is fine. She'll come to terms with everything that happened, although she still gets jumpy. Dean can't harm either her or me. She had bought a little house not far from her parents' and again, I'm settling in and I hope this is the last time I have to go through this. I hate moving from one place to another. I mark the furniture with my scent. *Mine. Mine. Mine.* I explore the house and climb on the windowsill and take in my surroundings.

In case you haven't noticed, this is a love story between the cat and his human, where the cat had to choose between what was right or wrong, sacrifice himself to save another. This might be something a dog might do. But as I said, we display our affection to our humans differently. This experience has changed me. It affected me as it affected Jane. I'm haunted by it. I still love Dean. He'll forever remain my human. I was a frightened kitten when he found me, crying for my mum and my siblings in the cold. He gave warmth and comfort. He saved my life. He rescued me, and for that, I owe him and will love him forever. I'll never forget him. I'm mourning for him as I watch the house sparrow. It's safe from my claws as the window is closed.

Note from the Author

If you enjoy what I write, you can help this little writer out by writing a review on Amazon or Goodreads or any platform of your choice. Reviews are the lifeline for authors and readers trust other readers. If you use social media, spread the word. It will be wonderful to have my book listed with others you have enjoyed.

Love,
J.S Ellis xx

You can sign up for my newsletter, and keep updated with new releases, offers, updates and giveaways.

Get a free short story when joining the list
https://joannewritesbooks.com

If you enjoyed this book you will enjoy!

In Her Words One night. One woman. One Man. One   Mystery.

While she seems to have it all, Sophie Knight is looking for more. When gorgeous and carefree Michael Frisk walks into her life, he offers the excitement and passion she desires.

Sophie is willing to risk everything she has. After all, she is used to concealing things from her husband—like her alcoholism, her unhappiness. But soon she has more to hide. She wakes up one morning in an alcoholic haze and finds bruises on her body, but has no recollection of what happened to her. Was she raped? When unsettling notes and mysterious phone calls start, Sophie wonders whom she should turn to. Is Michael the cause of the frightening things happening in her life, or is he the answer to her problems?

The Secret She Kept

She's dead. Why would she lie?

Days before her murder, Anthony's friend, Lottie, lent him her laptop. Curiosity getting the best of him, he clicks on a file and finds videos recorded by her in the year leading up to her death. Within those recordings, she exposes dark secrets someone will kill to keep hidden, and Lottie's toxic relationship with Anthony's long-time friend, Davian.

When Anthony's childhood friend, Davian is placed under arrest for the murder, Anthony refuses to believe he could do such a thing but Lottie was infatuated by Davian. More damning evidence piles up, Anthony wonders if it's possible a man he's known for most of his life has kept a sinister side of himself hidden.

Now, Anthony faces an impossible choice; turn the laptop over to the police and risk being accused of hindering the investigation, or try to solve the case himself. Lottie gave him the computer for a reason. There was something there she wanted him to see. Can he put the pieces of the puzzle together in time to uncover the killer?

The Rich Man

Her boyfriend vanished, but moving on could be murder...

Acey left without a word, leaving Elena alone to pick up the pieces of her broken heart. Determined not to be crushed by his betrayal, she forces herself to get over him.

Never did she fathom the unspeakable darkness closing in...

Sinclair Diamond breezes into her life like an answered prayer. Handsome. Wealthy. Charming. As he lovingly dotes on her, Elena finds herself falling for him.

But Sinclair has unspeakable secrets all his own.

Men in black suits trailing them. Shady business dealings. The odd chain of events surrounding his first wife's death. The more Elena learns about Sinclair, the more her apprehension builds. Yet when a ghost from her past reappears, Elena is forced to face a startling truth that could cost her everything.

Can she escape the web of deceit tightening around her? Or will she be the next to mysteriously disappear?

Lost and Found Book 1

Despite being polar opposites, Phoebe and Adele's friendship has stretched on for years. One a bubbly blonde, the other raven-haired and studious. They seem to have nothing in common, yet the bond between them is unbreakable.
Or so Phoebe thought.

She never believed Adele would hide anything from her until she sees her sneaking off with her handsome neighbour. Feeling betrayed, Phoebe begins to see cracks in their friendship she never noticed before.
Then, Adele vanishes.

Fearing for Adele's safety, Phoebe searches for clues about her disappearance. However, the deeper she digs, the more she realizes she didn't know Adele as well as she thought. Yet as revelations come to light, one mystery remains. What happened to Adele? And how is her disappearance connected to the stranger next door?

Hide and Seek Book 2

Hope is waning with Phoebe no closer to finding her best friend, Adele. Her suspicions involving her neighbour, Alan, have been cleared, leaving her no other hunches to pursue.

Until the letter arrives.

A message, written in Adele's hand, paints a picture of a side of her friend's life Phoebe never knew. Renewed with optimism that she is still alive, Phoebe launches back into the investigation. Among the pages of Adele's communications Phoebe finds evidence pointing to an unlikely suspect...

And yet another connection to Alan.

He seemed so concerned about the investigation, wanting to help in any way he could. Was the man next door a genuine ally? Or working to protect the real culprit?

The Confidant

Secrets have deadly consequences.

A part of him knew she was always lying, but he could change that. He could change her.

When charismatic Zoë first sits in Jason's salon chair, he can immediately tell they have a connection. Who wouldn't? She was smart, witty, and incredibly funny, everything someone could want in a budding friendship. But soon, Jason learns there is more to Zoë than meets the eye.

When lies are uncovered and secrets exposed, Jason must decide just how far he's willing to go in the name of friendship.

How far should he go to uncover the truth? If he digs too deep, could Jason lose the very person he's trying to keep?

When it all comes crashing to the light, and someone's very life hangs in the balance, will he regret what he's done? Or will Jason wish he had only done more?

Scan the code to buy the books

About the author.

J.S Ellis is a thriller author. She lives in Malta with her fiancé and their furbaby, Eloise. When she's not writing or reading, she's either cooking, eating cheese and chocolate, or listening to good music and enjoying a glass of wine or two.

Website https://joannewritesbooks.com
Facebook https://www.facebook.com/authorJ.SEllis/
Instagram @ author_j.sellis
Goodreads http://bit.ly/2P8a9xx
Pinterest: https://bit.ly/3iqBvrU
Amazon: https://amzn.to/30rbKSq
Bingebooks: https://bingebooks.com/author/j-s-ellis
Bookbub: https://www.bookbub.com/authors/j-s-ellis

Made in the USA
Columbia, SC
09 December 2021

50813845R00100